Little Jack

Michael Neece

Published by Michael Neece, 2021.

This is a work of fiction. Similarities to real people, places, or events are entirely coincidental.

LITTLE JACK

First edition. February 28, 2021.

Copyright © 2021 Michael Neece.

ISBN: 979-8201625535

Written by Michael Neece.

To the rebels, the rejects, and the outsiders. The ones that have stared down adversity and emerged victorious. To the lost and forgotten souls who paid their dues in rock bottom's basement. This book stands in honor of you.

Chapter 1

"**B**am! Pop!" You could hear the punches landing throughout the gym.

"Knock him out, Ace!" screamed a fat man from the bleachers.

"I got a carton on ya, Ace. Don't let me down," yelled another con who looked close to having a heart attack from all of the excitement.

"Bam! Smack!" Ace landed two more solid punches. Blood flew from his opponent's mouth as he crumbled to the canvas.

The crowd roared in the over packed gym as the loser's head connected with the mat. Screams and stomping feet raised the sound to an almost deafening proportion.

Saturdays were always the same at Turndale. Some guys had been down for over twenty years and didn't remember it being any different.

"Still undefeated huh, Ace?" The old timer said with a cough as Ace made his way out of the gym.

Ace walked through his congratulations to meet up with the fellas out on the yard. The fellas were glad to be friends with Ace. At six feet two inches tall and two hundred fifty pounds of solid muscle, he was an intimidating looking guy.

The fact that he hadn't lost a match in the entire four years and eleven months he had been at Turndale was a factor weighed into his popularity.

Out on the yard the day was cool with a shadowy overhead. The clouds didn't let the sun out but for a minute at a time. The breeze was a light one, bringing with it the occasional smell of cow manure from the nearby Illinois farms.

"Leaving here a champion, huh Ace?" Pops asked with a toothless grin before spitting a puddle of chew juice onto the ground. He had been at Turndale for close to thirty years, longer than anyone there. He knew he wasn't getting out either. The parole board always shot him down.

When he started his time, he acted like a wild-man and spent most of his first ten years in the hole. A stabbing here, giving a beating there, he was filled with hatred towards the world, but after that first ten years, Turndale became his home. He became adjusted to prison life. Pops was a well-respected convict among his peers.

"If I make it through next weekend, Pops," Ace answered.

"Eight days left. I can't wait until I get that short," Tom said. He had come in with Ace on the same bus. They became friends right away. Tom got twenty years for killing his wife for cheating on him. It wasn't his first time in prison and probably wouldn't be his last.

Turndale was built in the early nineteen hundreds and was meant to house the worst of the worst in Illinois. Ace Sampson didn't have any business being at Turndale. It was his boxing ability that landed him there. The warden at Turndale had brought him from a lower security prison when he came to take over.

"What are you going to do when you get out?" Pops asked.

"I'm going home to my woman and babies. Hell, I ain't seen them in five years. I would've been able to visit if the goddamn warden hadn't taken me with him when he transferred here. I wasn't even at that joint a week and I was gone."

"Yeah, that's wrong man. How many babies you got?" Bobby asked, one of his eyes burnt shut.

"Three."

"How old are they?" Everyone knew that Bobby's children were killed in a fire at his farm years ago. He turned to liquor and robbing banks shortly after.

"My boy is twelve. He was seven when I left. My girls were four when I left, so they're nine now. Twin girls."

"What's their names?"

"The girls are Tara and Tanya. My boy's name is Jack."

"Cherish them Ace," Bobby said. All the fellas could see the pain in his eyes. The pain of a man whose grief for a lost family caused his own near self-destruction.

"I do Bobby. I always do." Ace turned around at the sound of approaching keys jingling from a waist chain.

"Damn it," Pops said turning red. His shock of white hair blew in the light wind as he watched the approaching hack.

"Ace," the big, red bearded correctional officer yelled.

"Yeah," answered Ace, turning to face the guard.

"Come on, Warden wants to see you."

Ace looked at his friends, "Later, fellas."

"Later, Ace."

"Let's go," the hack urged.

"Comin' boss," Ace said as he walked in step behind the burly man in uniform.

"That's never good news," Pops said with a shake of his head as he spat on the ground in distaste.

"You're right about that," Bobby agreed.

"COME IN," THE WARDEN said when Ace reached the office.

"Yes, sir," was Ace's reply as he entered the room. The officer shut the door and waited outside.

"Have a seat," said the warden, without looking up from his paperwork. This wasn't Ace's first visit to the warden's office. He took his seat and looked at the walls. He was always interested in the pictures of long ago wardens that adorned those walls. Some of them were on horseback as if they were slave masters keeping order. Ace had been in that office on the same day, every year, since Turndale became his home. The week before Big Saturday.

Big Saturday was that day of the year when all the top boxers came to Turndale with their wardens for championship bouts. Local businessmen and connected thugs also visited the prison on that day for heavy betting.

Ace was undefeated four years running. That made Warden Brown very happy, not to mention the wealth he had amassed.

"You won again," Warden Brown said. It was a statement, not a question. His guards kept him informed.

"Yes, sir," Ace answered.

"Good. Now, your last match is next Saturday, Big Saturday, then you'll be going home on Monday."

"Yes, sir."

"All of the odds are in your favor. That's why I want you to throw your last match."

"What?" Ace asked loudly.

"You heard me."

"Why?"

"Why?" said the warden. "You're going to question me? Well, if you must know, it's so I can clean up."

"I'm undefeated, Warden."

"Exactly."

"I can't."

"Yes, you can! And you will! If you want to see your family again you will. I can make sure you get more time here, and then your life will be a living hell. Nobody will be there for your family either. It's your choice though, Ace. What's it going to be?"

Ace looked around at the walls, checking out the wardens of the past. Wondering if they were any different from the one sitting across from him. With a deep breath, he answered. "Okay, Warden. It's just a prison match. Whatever you want."

"I'm glad you made the right choice, Ace. I'll need you to go down in the fourth round. Is that understood?"

"Yes, sir."

"That will be all," the warden said with a disgusted look on his face.

Ace left the wardens office in despair.

"KIDS GET IN HERE. IT'S time to eat," Denise Sampson yelled, through her torn screen door to her twin girls who were in the front yard.

"Comin' Mama," Tara shouted.

"Comin' Mama," Tanya echoed.

"Where is Little Jack?" Denise asked the girls, frustrated.

"We haven't seen him," Tara answered.

"That boy is going to get it if he doesn't get in here real quick," Denise said while walking to the door.

"Jack! Jaaaccckkkk!" she screamed at the top of her lungs.

"He'll be home soon Mama," Tanya said, while nervously pulling and twisting her long, curly blond hair. Her deep blue eyes misty at the thought of her big brother in trouble again.

"You girls go ahead and eat. I'm going back to bed. You tell Little Jack I want to see him when he gets home. If he ever gets home."

"Okay Mama," the girls answered.

"And get those dishes done too."

"Yes, Mama."

When their mother left the room, Tara looked at Tanya and said, "Jack's in trouble again."

"I know it," Tanya said back.

"Mama's drunk again too."

"I know."

BANG! BANG! BANG! THE knocking on the door woke the little girls up. They were cuddled up to each other on the couch. They fell asleep on the couch most nights when their mother was drunk.

"Who is it?" Tanya asked.

"Police," came the answer from the other side.

"Go get Mama," Tara said to Tanya, who flew down the hall in the run down, three-bedroom shanty that was their home. The only home they ever knew.

Denise came into the living room with Tanya at her feet. Tara was standing by the door. Both girls could smell the alcohol on their mother, and secretly prayed that the policeman wouldn't take her away. Denise rubbed the sleep away from her eyes before answering the door with a groggy, "Hello."

On the other side of the door stood a tall police officer with his hand on the shoulder of none other than Little Jack.

"I didn't do nothin," Jack blurted out before the officer could say anything.

"Miss Sampson?" he asked.

"It's Mrs."

"Mrs. Sampson, is this your son?"

"Yes, it is officer. What's he done now?"

The officer could hear the anger in the woman's voice and knew the boy's trouble hadn't even begun yet. "Ma'am, we caught him fighting earlier. It was also past curfew."

Denise looked at Jack and ignoring the officer said, "I told you to be home in time for dinner."

Jack looked at the ground and shamefully said, "Sorry Mama."

"Who was he fighting?" She asked the officer.

"A couple of kids actually ma'am. Across town."

"Couple of kids!" Denise exclaimed. Her anger turning to concern. "Jack. Look at me."

Jack hesitantly looked at his mother. She gasped when she saw that his left eye was swollen, nearly shut. Her head dropped as she shook it from side to side.

"We're going to release him into your custody, ma'am."

"Thank you, Officer."

The officer looked at Little Jack. He squatted down to be eye level with him. "Jack, we don't want to catch you out past curfew again. No more fighting either. Okay?"

"Hell, they started it," was Little Jack's reply.

"Jack!" Denise yelled, her concern changing back to anger.

"Sorry," Little Jack said, once again staring back at the ground.

"Alright then," said the officer, "I'll be seeing you later."

"Thank you, sir," Denise said. "Boy, get in here," she whispered to Jack.

Jack hesitated again, considered bolting, but thought better of it. He'd put his Mama through too much already. Not that he thought the big man in the uniform had a chance at catching him on his own turf. "Yes Ma'am," Little Jack said as he entered the house.

After she shut the door, Denise said to the girls, "Go to your room." The girls didn't answer, just obeyed. They didn't want to get what Jack was getting ready to get.

Denise walked into the kitchen and grabbed 'The Switch' from the top of the refrigerator. "So, you want to be a big fighter like your father?" she asked as she walked towards her frightened son. He hated the sight of that God awful piece of willow. "Answer me! Do you want to be a big fighter like your father?"

"No Mama," Little Jack answered, backing up.

"Don't lie to me boy. You want to go to prison, be like your father. Big fighter."

"Mama, no," Jack pleaded.

Whack! The first hit of the switch landed across his left cheek. Jack dropped from the blow, but Denise kept hitting. Whack! Whack! Whack! All the slicing blows from the switch landed on Little Jack's backside as he balled up on the hard wood floor. He could feel the bloody wetness run down his cheek as he fought to block out the stinging blows he was receiving.

"Stop it, Mama!" The girls screamed. They had entered the room, scared, and crying. They had never heard their mother whip Jack so bad, or so long and hard.

Denise stopped at the sound of the twins. She was breathing heavily. As she came to her senses, she realized that she had blacked out during the beating.

Tara ran to Jack, followed by her sister. "Jack," the first girl said, crying. Little Jack looked up, with his left eye close to swollen shut and a fresh, welt-like gash on the right side of his face. The new gash was bleeding, but he said, "I'm alright."

Denise looked at her son as if waking from a dream. Seeing the lacerations on his face, dropped her to her knees. She covered her mouth with one hand and began to cry.

All three girls gathered around Jack, crying, and shaking as they hugged him. "It's alright Mama. It's okay girls."

"Baby, I'm sorry," Denise sobbed.

They all embraced each other hard. The pressure on Little Jack's back hurt him. He knew the cuts were bleeding, but just bit his lip and hugged back. With his shirt sticking to his back, he said again, "It's going to be okay, Mama. Everything is going to be better."

"I know Jack," Denise cried. "It will all be fine when daddy gets home," she said, regaining some composure. After wiping her eyes, she looked around at her run-down home. She couldn't wait to leave the place. "Yes," she thought, "everything will be fine next Monday."

All the girls went to bed as Jack went into the bathroom to wash up. When he finished doctoring himself, he made his way to the kitchen where a loaf of bread and cold meat loaf dinner awaited him. Pain shot through the left side of his face every time he chewed, but he didn't care. He was just glad that he would be reunited with his father soon.

Chapter 2

"**G**rampa," Little Jack said when he entered the bar.

"Jack," his grandfather greeted back.

"Got any work for me?" Jack asked.

"Why ain't you in school?" Grampa asked, then saw the boy's face as he came into the light. "God son, what happened to your face?"

"Got in a fight with the Campbells."

"All of them?" Grampa asked, amazed.

"Nah, just Bill and George," Jack answered, trying not to sound too proud.

"Son, they're both bigger than you. Get over here and let me take a look."

"Did you give 'em some work, Jack?" An old drunk Jack knew as Ed, asked.

"I whooped both of 'em," Jack stated, not hiding how proud he was anymore as he made his way over to his grandpa.

Grampa was proud of course. He taught Little Jack how to box. He'd taught Little Jack's father, Ace also. Grampa had seen a lot of the same traits that his son held in his grandson. They were both naturals, quick to pick up a move.

Ace's real name was Jack. He took the name Ace from an old friend, who died when they were young. That friend had always called him Ace. Three Jacks in a row. Little Jack had told himself that if he ever had a boy, he would name him Jack too.

"What did your Mama say?" Grampa asked.

"She wasn't too happy, but I took care of it." Jack wasn't going to tell his grandfather about the beating or the police. Mama had too many problems already. He knew things would be better when his daddy got out Monday.

"Got some wood needs choppin' out back," Grampa Jack said. "Should keep you busy till lunch."

"Yes sir. Then some lessons?"

"You got it boy. I got to get you ready in case three of them try to get you next time."

"I'm ready for three now," Jack said smiling.

"I'll bet you are," Ed chimed in with a laugh, blowing out smoke from his Pall Mall cigarette, his yellow teeth showing.

"Go on out boy. I'll call you for lunch," Grampa said.

"Yes sir," Jack said, walking out back to the wood pile.

When he was gone, the smile left the eldest Jack's face. He knew that the shiner might have been from the fight, but not the welt. He'd bet anything and everything he had that Denise did that in a fit of rage. The boy seemed all right so he wasn't going to push the issue. Ace would be home on Monday.

"That there's a good boy," Ed said before drowning himself with his beer. "It's normal for boys to be fighting."

Grampa Jack looked over at Ed and knew that he was right. "Yeah Ed, but it's the forties. You'd think these kids would be more civilized."

"WHATCHA DOIN?"

Jack swung around from chopping wood to see 'Dumb ol' Cindy Thompson' standing there looking at him. "God, how does she know to come out every time I'm out here," he thought to himself. "What does it look like I'm doing?" He said out loud.

"Well, I can tell that you're chopping wood, Jack."

"Then why'd you ask?"

"Just trying to make conversation. Heard the Campbell boys whooped ya last night."

"Nope."

"That's just what I heard, but I saw Bill and George. They both had black eyes. George got a tooth knocked out too."

"Fightin's not for little girls to be talking about." Grampa had taught him that.

"I am eleven years old Jack Sampson. One year younger than you," Cindy yelled, angry at Jack for treating her like a child.

"Well, I have to finish this work."

"Okay Jack," Cindy said. She then walked home, which was next door.

Cindy was poor and didn't have a daddy. At least she'd never seen him before and didn't know who he was. Jack felt sorry for her because he knew what it was like to be without a dad.

"Time for lunch boy," Grampa Jack said from the back door. He looked over and saw Cindy approaching her back door. "Poor girl," he said. Grampa Jack owned the house next door. Cindy's mother was late on rent as usual. The only reason he hadn't kicked her out on her worthless bottom was because of that sweet little girl. "How come she ain't in school?"

"I don't know. Didn't ask."

"Come on. I made some sandwiches."

CINDY WATCHED FROM the window of her dirty kitchen as Little Jack disappeared into the bar. She had gone to school that morning, but when she heard about the fight and saw that Little Jack wasn't there, she knew where he would be. So, she played sick to get home.

HANK WILLIAMS WAS PLAYING on the new juke box when Little Jack entered the bar to eat his lunch. He'd heard this one before but was still filled with chills. Hank always done that to him. He grabbed a stool next to Ed and began eating.

"Why'd your Mama let you stay home from school?" Grampa asked.

"Because she didn't want the social services people being called on account of my eye," Little Jack answered, without looking up from his lunch.

"God forbid that. You know how them people are," Ed said.

After Little Jack and Grampa finished lunch, Grampa had Julie, the waitress, watch the bar.

Out back Grampa was showing some different stances to Little Jack. Cindy was peaking from the dirty kitchen window. She was in love with Jack Sampson. "I'm going to marry him someday," she thought out loud.

When the lessons for the day were finished, Grampa and Little Jack sat on the back porch. The sun was beginning its descent, letting the night take over for its temporary reign. The wind moved through the long weeds that were scattered throughout the back yard, around assorted piles of junk. It was a warm evening with the smell of the nearby river overpowering any other smell in the vicinity.

"Your daddy will be home Monday."

"Yeah, I can't wait."

"Five years is a long time to be away from your family. Do you know why your daddy went to prison?"

"For fightin'," Little Jack answered.

"No, for fightin' with the police Little Jack. There's a big difference."

"Why'd he fight with the police?" Little Jack asked. It was something that he'd wanted to know for a long time.

"Because one of them was disrespecting your mother."

"My Mama?"

"Yes."

"Why?"

"Jealous, I guess."

"What happened?"

"Well," Grampa Jack said. He looked around and noticed a couple of rabbits gathered around the big oak tree in his yard. He hadn't talked to Little Jack about this before, but figured he was old enough now. With a sigh, he told the story. "Your Mama and Daddy went out dancing one night at a bar. There were four off-duty Sheriff's deputies at this bar. To make a long story short, one of the deputies talked trashy to your mother and then grabbed her. That's all it took. Your daddy put it to all four of them."

"Four of them?"

"Yep," Grampa answered with a smile. "I taught him how to box just like I'm teachin' you."

"I know," Little Jack said.

"It's a shame he had to go to prison. He would have been Champion. Still might be when he gets out. They say he is undefeated up there."

"I'm going to be Champion."

"Ha, Ha," Grampa laughed. "You sure will, if you stick with me kid."

"You were going to be Champion, weren't ya, Grampa?"

"That's what they say. At least 'til the shrapnel tore my knee to hell. That's life though son. When your country calls for you, you got to go. My daddy died while I was over there. He left me this bar and a couple of houses. He got it all from fightin' and runnin' 'shine. He used to run this whole county."

"Moonshine," Little Jack said proudly. He'd heard many stories about the prohibition days.

"Yep."

They sat in silence for a moment. Grampa sighed and Little Jack stared off in the distance. "Grampa?"

"Yes Jack?"

"What was your Mama like?"

Grampa didn't answer at first. Little Jack looked up to see that the old man was smiling. "Well, Jack, my Mama was the kindest and one of the most loved women around these parts. Everybody in town knew that if they had a problem, they could come to Jenny Sampson. It was the women folk mostly. She delivered so many babies around these parts for so many years. Why, she even delivered your daddy."

"Well, what happened to her?"

"She fell sick one winter. A lot of people did that year." Grampa paused as he went back to a painful time. "She never pulled out of it."

"Oh," said Little Jack, bowing his head.

"Mama loved the Lord, Jack. I never was worried about her. I knew as soon as she passed, she went straight on up to heaven where she belonged."

They sat and talked for a good forty-five minutes before Jack realized what time it was getting to be. He didn't want to have a repeat of the night before. "Well Grampa, I better be heading home. Don't want to be late for supper."

"Be careful Jack. If more than one of the Campbell boys come at ya, make sure you pick up an equalizer."

"Alright Grampa."

Grampa watched Jack walk through his backyard on his way home and thought about how nice it would be to have Denise and the grand babies living close by in one of his houses. He had asked her to move into one when Ace went to prison, but she was too proud to take charity from anyone, including family. Grampa Jack smiled as he watched Little Jack pick up a heavy stick from the edge of his yard and test it. He guessed he wanted to have the equalizer ready in case he found unwanted company on the walk home.

Chapter 3

You could feel the tension in the prison. Every Big Saturday was filled with adrenaline. Not only did the wardens from every prison in the state have their bets in, but the local thugs, businessmen and convicts had theirs as well.

Ace hadn't told anyone what was discussed in the Warden's office the week before. He didn't give it much thought after the first day. He knew what he had to do.

"Are you ready?" Pops asked. He always escorted Ace to the ring. He took pride in being his corner man.

"Let's go," Ace said, standing up. Despite all his prior experience, Big Saturday always made him nervous. His was the last match of the evening. The main event. Returning champion five years running was something that hadn't been done before. The closest was four, back in thirty-five. If Ace won tonight, he would be the first to win five years straight.

The wardens had a private box of their own. The inmates had most of the bleachers, with the thugs and businessmen taking up part of the rest. The correctional officers were scattered about the gym. They, too, had money riding on the fight.

When Ace entered the gym, he was shocked at the first sight of his opponent. The crowd came alive and loud as he made his way to the ring. Mostly, the convicts could be heard screaming and cheering on their boy "Damn, he's big," Ace thought as he locked eyes with his adversary, who was already standing in the middle of the ring.

Ace blocked out the noise in the gym as he entered the ring. He figured the man must be six feet, six inches tall, and solid as a petrified

Redwood log. His neck and arms were as thick as tree trunks. "Mean lookin' son of a bitch," Ace thought, as he walked to the middle of the ring.

The two men touched gloves. The noise from the crowd got even louder. Ace could feel his adrenaline rise.

"Ding!" the bell sounded. Both men flew at each other.

"Whop!" Ace's first punch landed under the big man's left eye. The big man bounced back as if he didn't even feel it. As he dodged and weaved, Ace could have sworn that he heard the big man laugh. Round and round they circled each other in the ring, each man bobbing and weaving around the other's hard swings.

"Swoosh!" the big man swung a hard, right hook. The punch bouncing off Ace's head. Not a solid connection, but enough to let Ace know he better get serious.

"Pop! Pop!" Ace countered with two jabs. The big man stumbled.

"Ding! Ding!" The first round was over.

Both men went to their corners. The cheers continued for Ace, obviously the crowd favorite. "That was your round Ace," Pops said as he rubbed Ace's shoulders. He squirted some water into his mouth and said, "Spit." Ace spit, breathing heavy and ready for round two.

"Ding!" both men flew at each other again "Tack!" the big man landed a jab on Ace's chin.

"Slam! Bam!" Ace recovered and countered with two of his own. He stepped back and blocked another incoming punch from the big man. Ace saw an opening and landed one with his power, left hand to the jaw. The big man hit the canvas hard.

The crowd snapped. "ONE! TWO!" The ref began his count after getting Ace to his corner. "THREE! FOUR!" The big man got up. "Are you alright?" the ref asked.

"Yes," the big man answered through his mouthpiece. He nodded his head, staring at Ace evilly.

"Fight!" the ref yelled. The two men squared off again. The big man danced around, more cautious of Ace's left hand. Ace moved in for a jab, landed it and stepped back as the bell sounded, ending round two.

Over in Ace's corner, Pops gave him his usual pep talk, yelling in his ear over the roar of the crowd. Ace heard something about faking with the left, but he wasn't really paying attention. As he smelled the blood in the air, he looked up at the Warden. When Ace locked eyes with the warden, he smiled. As the bell sounded for round three, Warden Brown looked as if he was going to be sick.

Round three ended with both men about even. They exchanged vicious blows with each other.

Round four started with Ace running into the middle of the ring. He threw a fake right jab, followed by a hard left. The big man stumbled back, but Ace was on him. Ace took his time and was cautious. The big man tried to block Ace's next left jab, so Ace turned and landed a hard right to the man's open ribs. When the big man went to block the next body shot, he let his guard down for the last time. Ace, picking his shot well, gave the big man his hardest left to the jaw. As the big man started to go down, Ace landed a right upper cut that could be heard over the crowd's screams.

"Boom!" the big man hit the canvas.

"Go to your corner!" the ref yelled. "ONE! TWO! THREE!"

"He ain't getting up!" Pops yelled to Ace when he got back to his corner.

"FOUR! FIVE! SIX!"

"You did it, Ace!" Pops exclaimed, excitedly. "Five years runnin'!"

"Yeah, I did it alright," Ace said as he looked up towards the warden. "I sure did."

"TEN! You're out!"

The gymnasium erupted. "ACE! ACE! ACE!" The convicts chanted.

Ace made his way back to the locker room. He received pats on the back as he went. Pops was so happy and excited it was a wonder he didn't keel over from a stroke or heart attack.

IN FIFTEEN MINUTES, the gym was quiet. The on-duty officers had escorted all the inmates back to their quarters. All the men that were free to leave had left the institution.

The warden entered the locker room with three, angry-looking officers. "Get out of here!" Warden Brown yelled at Pops.

Pops looked at Ace. Ace just nodded his head for Pops to leave.

When Pops left the locker room, Ace looked at the warden. Smiling, he asked, "What took you so long?"

"Get him," Warden Brown ordered. All three officers pulled their batons.

"Ha, "Ace said, under his breath while taking a defensive stance. It was the last word he ever said.

"WHERE'S ACE AT? HE'S been gone all afternoon," Bobby had asked later that day.

"I'm telling you, he's in trouble," Pops said. "I should have never left him."

"He'll be alright," Bobby said. He didn't know what was going on but didn't want the fellas to worry so much.

They never saw Ace again. That night, after the evening chow, word hit the yard. Ace had died in the prison hospital. The word going around was that even though he won the fight, one of the big man's punches had erupted some type of blood vessel in his head.

The fellas knew better. Pops more than the rest. He was there when the warden walked in. After doing so much time, he could read eyes better than anyone.

"He was supposed to lose that match," Pops stated.

"We don't know that" Bobby said.

"We do know a punch didn't kill him," Tom said.

They were out on the yard while matches were going on. New Saturday. Everybody else was in the gym, betting on a new champion. The fellas passed. They were sick of boxing.

Chapter 4

Sunday morning found Little Jack up early. Earlier than he could remember in all his twelve years. The girls were still asleep, so Jack crept down the hall of the old house on his tiptoes. He made it to the front door, looked over at the kitchen and thought of breakfast. He decided to pass. He didn't want to wake the girls.

Out on the porch, he closed the front door as quietly as possible. The sun was just coming up. He took in the sight with a deep breath. "That's the first time I've ever seen the sunrise," he thought before stepping off the porch.

He walked to the shed on the side of the house and opened the door. He had to be quiet with the old, rusty thing. He was worried that the sound would wake the girls if he wasn't careful.

Inside the shed, he climbed up on the work bench, reminding himself to oil the shed door when he left. On the bench, he reached up into the rafters and grabbed what he came for. Two rods and reels that he had worked hard for. Most of his money from working for Grampa Jack went towards getting them. The rest of the money went for candy for his sisters and a box of chocolates for his mother on her birthday.

"Tomorrow," he thought, "Me and daddy will be going fishing."

Little Jack stayed in the shed for the better part of an hour, cleaning up. He wanted to make sure that when his daddy came home, he'd like the workplace. When he thought everything was good enough, he oiled the old rusty door hinges.

After inspecting his work, and making sure the door didn't squeak anymore, he put the oil back and left the shed. His stomach was growling as he walked back towards his house.

He could smell the biscuits and gravy when he got to the front door. When he walked inside, he saw his sisters on the couch.

"Little Jack," they said in unison. They were always doing things like that.

"Where have you been?" Denise asked from the kitchen.

"I was out cleaning the shed," Little Jack answered. Then asked, "What's for breakfast?"

Denise didn't answer. Instead, she asked another question. "Were you out all night?"

"No Mama."

"Don't lie to me Jack."

"I'm not lying Mama."

"He's not lying Mama," Tara cut in, saying, "I heard him go out this morning."

"I was trying to be quiet, so I wouldn't wake anybody up," Jack explained.

"Okay Jack," Denise said suspiciously. "Go and wash up. We'll be eating as soon as the taters are done fryin'."

"Yes, Mama," Jack answered before walking off to the bathroom.

AFTER BREAKFAST, LITTLE Jack changed for church. The girls were getting their bath while Mama was changing in her room, staring at her reflection in the mirror.

She was an attractive female with long, flowing blond hair. The girls had inherited her hair. Little Jack had followed his daddy with his light brown hair. They all had the bluest of blue eyes. As she looked in the mirror, she was happy to see that her figure hadn't changed much since Big Jack left. She was about the only person that didn't call him Ace. She wasn't worried about losing him. She knew she still had it. Big Jack had always fallen head over heels for her. All the boys did, growing up, but Ace was the one she chose. It wasn't because he never lost a fight either. That's all the other girls cared about, but not Denise. Her father was a fighter, and all fighting did for him was get him killed. No, Denise was in love with Big Jack because he could have had any girl in the county. Instead, he kept after her for two whole years. She turned him down the whole time and looking back was surprised he waited as long as he did.

After they were married and the kids came along, he gave up brawling. He boxed in the ring still but gave up the bare-knuckle matches for cash.

Denise looked at her hair closely in the mirror. "If the damn police wouldn't have been at the bar acting the way they were, he never would have got sent away." She had always told herself that he did the right thing. He did. "Oh well," she thought, "it will all be over tomorrow."

"Okay, girls, get out of the tub and get dressed for church or we're going to be late," she yelled from her room.

"We are Mama," Tanya yelled back.

Little Jack was reading his bible in the living room, waiting on the girls. He always had to wait on them. He needed this time to memorize some verses for Sunday school anyway. He had three more memorized before the three women of the house were ready.

When they were all about to walk out the door, there came a knock from the other side of it.

"Who could that be on a Sunday morning?" Denise asked while walking over to the door. The kids followed and everyone's heart dropped when she opened the door. It was the same officer that brought Little Jack home the night of the fight. Denise looked at Little Jack. "I knew you were out all night."

"No, I wasn't Mama. I swear." He was afraid that he was going to be in trouble anyway.

"Don't swear, Little Jack," Denise said.

"No, Mrs. Sampson," the cop cut in, "this isn't about Little Jack. I'm afraid I have some bad news."

"What is it?" she asked in a scared, almost child-like voice. All the anger she had just expressed toward her son was gone.

"I think we should speak in private," the officer said, looking at the children.

"Girls, stay in the house," she said in her motherly tone.

"Mama," the girls cried. They were scared. Tears were already flowing down their rosy, red cheeks.

Denise ignored them and said, "Jack, come on." She might have been hard on him, but he had been the man of the house for the last five years. The strongest person out of all of them.

The officer couldn't look at Denise, so he kept his eyes locked onto Little Jack's. "I'm afraid Ace is dead."

"No!" Denise screamed. Her hand came up to her mouth. "No!" she sobbed hysterically. She turned around and went into the house, leaving Jack outside with the officer. Little Jack closed the door behind her.

"What is it, Mama?" Tara asked. She was scared when she saw her mother's condition.

"Daddy's dead," she blurted out before she realized what she was saying. Both girls began to sob and ran to their mother.

Back out on the porch, Little Jack was in shock, but held strong. He didn't cry. "How did it happen?"

"Boxing," the officer said. "They had Big Saturday up there yesterday. You know sometimes a person gets hit and that's it, son."

Little Jack tightened up when he heard the officer call him son. Wasn't it these guys who got his daddy sent away in the first place?

The officer went on speaking. It was a lot easier with the boy's mother gone, but still a hard task all the same. "The prison had your mother down as next of kin in case of an accident, but when they didn't have a number..."

"We don't have a phone." Little Jack was embarrassed about that. Most of the kids at school had phones.

"Well, the prison called down here to us."

"Thanks for coming," Little Jack said. He was done with this conversation.

"Man, this kid is tough," the officer thought. "I'm really sorry, Little Jack."

"Thank you for coming," Little Jack said again as he left. Little Jack went back inside. The girls were crying hysterically. It took all he had not to join in with them. He knew he had to be strong. He comforted them and put them all to bed. There wouldn't be any church today. His mother and sisters cried themselves to sleep.

Little Jack went into his bedroom and grabbed an envelope out of his dresser drawer. He changed out of his church clothes and put the envelope in his pocket. As he was leaving, he wrote a note in case his mother woke up. The note said that he went for a walk.

He left the house, walked past the shed, through the yard and into some trails at the end of their property. He took a smaller trail on the right that led to the river. Thinking about things a twelve-year-old should never have to think about, he walked until he reached his special spot.

The spot was on a small cliff that dropped off into the river. The only sounds Jack ever heard at this spot was birds, an occasional ground squirrel, and the fresh smelling, running water below. Today was especially peaceful. It was a warm sunny day. The trees kept most of the sun to themselves, not sharing much with Jack. He felt warm, but tired as he sat on the edge of the cliff and pulled the envelope out of his pocket.

He opened the envelope at the tear and pulled out the letter inside.

LITTLE JACK,

How are you? I hope fine and well. I got your letter just a few minutes ago and couldn't wait to get word back to you. I'm glad to hear you are taking care of your Mama and sisters like I asked you to.

I was surprised to hear that you saved up for some fishing poles. I'm looking forward to going fishing with you when I get home. In your spare time, you should find us a good spot.

I'll be home soon, Little Jack. Tell your sisters and your Mama that I send my love.

Take care son. I'm proud of you.

Love, Dad

LITTLE JACK HAD TEARS running down his cheeks when he finished reading the last letter his father had sent him.

"I've got a spot right here daddy," he said in a low, grief filled voice. The tears began to flow.

He sat at his spot for a long time. Until the tears stopped and dried up. He eventually got up and climbed down the path that led to a lower bank. The water was calmer here and easier to reach. He checked his reflection in the water to make sure no one could tell that he had been crying. When he was satisfied, he followed his path back home.

CINDY MADE IT TO THE spot while Little Jack was still sitting there. She knew he hadn't heard her because she was sure to keep quiet. She heard at Grampa Jacks bar what had happened. The word was all over town. Ace was dead. When Denise showed up at the bar with Tara and Tanya, Grampa had asked about Jack.

"He left a note saying he was going for a walk," Denise had answered.

Cindy knew where he would be. She had followed Jack out to this spot before.

As she watched Little Jack sitting there, she couldn't approach him. When he got up to leave, she noticed that he had dropped something. She watched as he walked down and looked at the river. She thought he was going to jump until he turned around and left. When she felt safe that he wouldn't be back, she walked over to his spot.

She saw that it was an envelope that he had dropped. Cindy picked it up and sat down. As she read the letter, tears ran down her face. Now Little Jack didn't have a daddy either.

THE FUNERAL WAS HELD on a cloudy day. The rain was drizzling down. Grampa Jack was staring at the ground with his umbrella in one hand. His cane was in the other. Little Jack was standing close enough to his Grampa that the rain wasn't getting on him.

The preacher was talking, but Grampa wasn't listening. He had buried the only woman he had ever loved and now he was burying his only child. So many memories, so many years. Ace had won his five years in a row, but it killed him. "Is it my fault?" Grampa thought. "I taught him. I raised him that way." He looked down at Little Jack. "Is he going to end up the same way?"

Little Jack was in a daze. His daddy was getting ready to be buried. Out of all the kids at school, the only one who showed up was Cindy Thompson. He looked over at her. She was crying. Everybody was crying but him and Grampa. She looked so sad. "Maybe she isn't so bad after all," he thought.

Chapter 5

It was the last day of school for the year. Four more hours to go. It was lunchtime. "Last lunch here," Little Jack thought. He would go to middle school next year. He wasn't worried about it, but his friend, Junior Pratchett was. Junior's brother had started middle school last year and had his head flushed in the toilet by some older kids.

"I don't want to go," Junior said for what seemed like the hundredth time that day. He was the only boy that ate lunch with Little Jack. The other boys didn't bother him when he was with Little Jack.

"I'd like to see someone try and flush my head down the toilet," Little Jack said while chewing on his sandwich.

Junior Pratchett threw his sandwich on his tray. "Little Jack, I know that you are tough, but when four or five of them guys come at you, you're going to get your head dunked." Junior was passionate when it came to things he knew about.

Little Jack swallowed his food and looked at his friend. He liked to get Junior worked up. Looking in his eyes, he said, "If four or five of them, by some crazy miracle, did get me…I'd be sure to get all four or five of them, one at a time, by the end of the day."

"Oh, oh, Little Jack, you don't understand shit. You're just going to have to find things out the hard way."

"Excuse me?" Mrs. Hazel cut in.

"Yes, Mrs. Hazel," Junior answered.

"What did you just say?"

"Nothin'," Junior answered. His eyes bugged out when he realized that she might have heard his curse. Looking at his friend's pudgy red face, Little Jack almost burst out laughing.

"Yes, you did," Mrs. Hazel said in a stern voice.

"No, I didn't. I swear."

"Don't swear Mr. Pratchett. You've done enough of that for one day. Come with me please."

"I didn't do anything!" Junior pleaded. It was just a matter of time before the tears began to fall.

"Come on," Mrs. Hazel said again before walking away.

"Aww man," Junior said as he got up, fighting the tears.

"I'll see you after school," Little Jack said.

Junior gave his friend a look of confirmation before following the teacher to the principal's office.

The rest of the day in school was no problem for Little Jack. It was after school that the drama began to unfold for the little scrapper.

"What happened?" Little Jack asked Junior after school. They were on the front walk at the school and Junior was getting his bike from the bike rack. Little Jack had a bike, but someone had stolen it. His Grampa had bought him that one and his mother couldn't afford to get him another.

"Someone would just steal it again if I was able to get you one anyway," she had said. Junior didn't hold it against him. They always walked home. Junior would just push his bike next to Little Jack.

"What do you mean, what happened?" Junior asked his friend.

"You know what I mean. What happened when you left with Mrs. Hazel?"

"Oh that," Junior said. He walked about ten more steps before he answered. "Got paddled." His head was held high. A strut was added to his walk.

Neither boy spoke for a minute. They crossed the street. Junior was pushing his bike. Little Jack was walking next to him.

Junior Pratchett was taller than Little Jack. He was a lot fatter also. The other kids picked on him because of his weight, but not Jack.

"You don't believe me, do you?" Junior asked after an unnerving minute of silence.

"I didn't say that" Little Jack answered."

"You don't have to say so. I've known you forever and you think I'm lying."

Little Jack didn't say anything. The boys kept walking. Junior was stealing, side long glances at his friend. He was the first one to break the silence.

"Ten swats," Junior said.

"Ten swats?" Jack asked.

"That's how many times I got swatted."

"Who did it?"

"Mr. Weaver," Junior answered. "He is the principal."

"Did they call your Mama first?"

"No. Why?"

"Because they have to."

"What makes you say they have to call your Mama first?"

"It's school policy. When Mr. Jackson was principal, he paddled one of the older Campbell boys."

"So."

"Well, when old man Campbell found out about it, he came to the school and whooped Mr. Jackson really good."

"I ain't never heard of that one, Little Jack."

"Well, it's true."

As the boys walked, Little Jack watched Junior out of the corner of his eye. He could tell that his fat friend was in deep thought.

"Well," Junior began. "They might have called without me knowing about it."

"I doubt it," Little jack said.

"How do you know it's policy? You ain't never been paddled."

"The only reason I ain't got paddled is because we ain't got a phone," Little Jack said.

"You ain't got a phone?" Junior asked.

"No. Got a problem with it?"

"No."

"Anyway, every time they tried to paddle me, they would want to call home, but couldn't."

"Really," Junior exclaimed. He looked at his friend with even more admiration.

"Yep," Jack answered proudly. "I remember one time, Mrs. Cooper wanted me paddled badly, but I heard Mr. Weaver ask her if she knew who my Daddy was."

"What'd she say?"

"She didn't even answer. She just said that she forgot."

"Ha, Ha," Junior laughed.

"I'm just glad they don't have Grampa's number. I don't know what he might have said. Probably just would have told them to go to Hell. I wasn't willing to take the risk though."

"So, what did they do instead of paddling?" Junior asked.

"Give me a note for Mama to sign."

"I'll bet she whooped ya, didn't she?"

"Nope."

"Why not?"

"She never seen the notes. I'd just sign her name and turn it back in. Passed every time."

"Really!" Junior said again. "If I ever get a note, you and I are gonna talk."

"No sweat. All I need is a copy of your Mama's signature and I can put it on the note."

"Cool."

"Are you sore?"

"What for?" Junior asked.

"From the paddling, idiot."

"Oh... No, it was only ten licks."

"I think ten licks would hurt."

"You still don't believe me, do you?"

"Well, Johnny Rivers was in the nurse's station, next to the principal's office, when you were in there," Little Jack said looking at his friend out of the corner of his eye again. He smiled when he saw the color leave Junior's face. They were just passing the old gas station.

"What did he hear?" Junior asked, sounding genuinely worried.

Johnny Rivers wasn't in the nurse's station as far as Little Jack knew, but it was working on Junior. "He didn't hear any paddling."

They turned left, towards the park, when they heard her scream. Whatever Junior was about to say was forgotten. Little Jack could see a group of boys in a circle. There was someone in the middle of the circle trying to get something back from the boys, but they were playing keep away. When the girl screamed again, Little Jack knew all he needed to know.

"That's Cindy," he said as he took off running.

"Really!" Junior screamed, hopping on his bike to catch up with his friend.

"Give it back!" Cindy screamed at her tormentors. Five older boys surrounded her. The three Campbells, Bill, George, and Freddy. The other two boys were Skinners, Ralph, and Tim.

When Little Jack got close enough and saw what was going on, he didn't like it. The Campbells and the Skinners had Cindy's bag and were throwing it back and forth between each other. Cindy was trying her hardest to catch the bag but was far from getting close every time.

Junior made it to the scene just in time to see Little Jack grab George Campbell by the shoulder, spin him around and sock him a good one in the nose.

"Wow!" Junior said.

Little Jack took a step back and hit George again, this time with a left hook. George spun around and hit the ground, unconscious.

"Come on!" Little Jack screamed, taking a stance that his Grampa had taught him.

"You son of a bitch!" yelled Bill Campbell before dropping Cindy's bag.

Looking hard into the bigger boy's eyes, Little Jack motioned for him to bring it on with his fists.

Tim Skinner started walking around, intending to blind side Little Jack. Junior saw the move and wasn't going for it. He jumped off his bike and with rage, blasted the Skinner boy with a right. The punch caught him in the temple.

Little Jack, seeing that Bill was distracted for a second, jumped on his opportunity. He hit him in the throat with a solid punch, followed by a swift kick to the groin. Bill Campbell fell to the ground with a sound coming out of him that Little Jack had never heard before.

Cindy grabbed her bag and took a couple of steps back, away from the action. Junior had moved on top of Tim Skinner. He was blindly landing punches on him. Ralph Skinner ran up and was about to kick Junior in the face until Cindy screamed. Little Jack, hearing the scream, saw Ralph and jumped in the boy's way, blocking the kick.

Freddy Campbell, the oldest and meanest of the bunch, came around with a left hook to Little Jack's left eye. Little Jack didn't see the punch coming. He stumbled from the blast. Ralph saw Little Jack stumble and hit him with a right jab. Little Jack stumbled further backwards, falling over Junior and Tim.

Junior looked over at Little Jack as if the intrusion had snapped him back to his senses.

Little Jack shook his head and stood up, ready for combat. Junior stood up and faced Ralph Skinner. He picked a stance that Little Jack had taught him.

"Fat ass, want some of me?" Ralph asked before spitting some chew juice on the ground. He wiped his mouth with the back of his hand and knuckled up.

"You're gonna pay now, Little Jack Sampson," Freddy Campbell said. "You're lucky I wasn't there last time when my brothers whooped ya."

"Ha!" Little Jack said as he waved the bigger boy on with his hands.

"AAAAAHHH!" Freddy yelled as he charged. Little Jack fake kicked with his left leg. The bigger boy's instincts made him throw his hands down to block.

"Whop! Whop!" Little Jack landed a left and a right. Both shots connected hard.

Junior Pratchett wasn't so lucky. Ralph landed two punches to every one that Junior threw. Junior was starting to think he was going to get whooped when he got a break. Junior sent a left hook towards Ralph but received a hard right jab. Ralph made the mistake of trying to follow through with a kick. That's when the break came in. Junior caught the leg, lifted it up, and slammed down onto the other boy.

Freddy Campbell was swinging wildly, but for the life of him he couldn't connect with the younger boy. This frustrated him, so he tried harder. It wasn't long after that that the younger boy's dodging and weaving had the older boy wore out. Little Jack stepped in with another fake kick, followed by a jab to the stomach. When he saw his wide-open shot, Little Jack came from downtown with an upper cut. The last punch knocked Freddy off his feet, into the air, and onto his back.

"Ooh," Cindy winced when she saw that one.

Breathing heavily, Little Jack looked over to see Junior pounding Ralph Skinner. "Alright Junior," he said.

Junior looked around, out of focus. Finally, he caught Little Jack's eye. Little Jack nodded and Junior got up.

The defeated boys started helping each other up. "Just wait!" Bill yelled while walking away with the other boys. He was holding onto his side as if his ribs were broken.

"Anytime!" Junior screamed, out of breath.

Little Jack didn't say anything. He turned and looked at Cindy.

"Are you alright?" She asked Little Jack.

Little Jack nodded his head and still out of breath said, "Yeah." Then he asked, "You?"

"Yeah," she answered.

"I'm gonna have a black eye," Junior said.

Little Jack looked over at his friend. He saw he wasn't lying. Junior's left eye was swollen and puffy.

"Thanks," Little Jack said.

"No sweat," Junior said back and then added. "You're gonna have a shiner too."

"I'm used to it," Little Jack said.

They all three walked to the tracks. Junior excitedly talked about the fight all the way. "Well, so long," he said.

"Later," Little Jack said. "And watch your back."

"I will," Junior said, walking away. "Hey, you know that thing we was talking about?"

"What?" Little Jack asked.

"About school," Junior said.

"Oh, yeah," Little Jack realized that he was talking about the paddling that never happened.

"Let's keep that between us."

"Sure," Little Jack said with a smile.

Junior departed. He lived to the left of the tracks, Jack and Cindy lived to the right.

"I'll walk you home," Little Jack told Cindy.

"Thank you."

"I just want to make sure those guys don't catch up with you and start more trouble."

"I meant, thank you for saving me."

"Ah, don't sweat it."

They made their way down a winding alley. When they got to a big oak tree right around the corner from Grampa's bar and Cindy's house, she stopped.

"I've got something in my shoe," she said. She put one hand on Jack's shoulder to balance herself while she dumped a rock out. "It's my birthday," she said, looking into Little Jack's eyes. Her hand was still on his shoulder. "I'm twelve now."

"Happy Birthday," Jack said.

Cindy closed her eyes and leaned forward. The kiss was quick and on its mark. Right on Jack's lips.

Jack didn't know what hit him at first, but when he did, he got all warm inside.

Cindy stepped back with a smile on her face. She giggled when she saw that Little Jack was beet red.

"That wasn't so bad...was it?"

"I, yeah...uh, I gotta go," Little Jack stammered before turning around and running full speed back down the alley.

Cindy watched him disappear and kept smiling. She hummed as she walked the rest of the way home.

Neither one of them knew it would be a long time before they saw each other again.

Chapter 6

Jack ran for a full minute before he was out of breath. He was on a wooded trail not far from his house. It was familiar territory.

He leaned up against a tree as he focused on catching his breath. "Man, she just kissed me," he thought. It was the first time he had been kissed by another girl besides his mother and sisters.

"It wasn't that bad," he mused before laughing out loud. Smiling, he closed his eyes and pictured the kiss again. Her lips were warm, and her breath was sweet. He pictured the kiss, over and over. He liked it and wondered why he ran.

With his wind finally back, he sighed Cindy's full name before starting his walk back home.

As he made his way around the backyard, he could hear the twins playing up in front.

"What are you girls doing?" Little Jack asked when he got the girls in sight.

"AAHHHH!" they yelled. "Jack, you scared us."

"Ha, Ha," he laughed.

"We're playin, Jack," Tara said. They were sitting in the dirt by the front porch, playing with some of Little Jack's old toy cars. A couple of regular old tomboys covered in dirt from head to toe.

"What happened to your eye?" Tara asked.

"Nothin'," Jack answered. "Just got hit playin ball. Where's Mama?"

"She's in bed," Tara answered.

"Drunk again," Tanya said.

"Looks like we'll have to fix our own dinners again," Tara said.

"No, I'll fix it," Little Jack said.

"What are you gonna fix?" Tanya asked.

"Oh, I'll think of something."

"Chicken, Jack, pleeaasse," Tanya pleaded.

"Chicken, chicken, chicken," Tara chimed in.

"Alright," Jack cut in, not being able to take the noise anymore. "But I want you to know that you're spoiled."

"Thank you," both girls said happily. They thanked him for the chicken, not for the spoiled comment he had made.

"I love you Jack," Tara said.

"I love you Jack," Tanya said.

"I love you too," Jack said back to them. "I'm going to go cook. When it's done, I'll holler for you two to come in and get cleaned up. Okay?"

"Okay Jack," Tara said.

"Okay Jack," Tanya said.

"Alright girls," Jack said and disappeared into the house. He had been cooking for the girls and himself a lot lately. Mama was always drunk. Daddy dying was very hard on her. Jack understood. He didn't mind all that much.

Little Jack washed his hands and got down to business. A smile stayed on his face as he worked. Cindy Thompson's image invaded his thoughts and mind. Those beautiful green eyes and blondish brown hair. She was a couple of inches shorter than him. "Oh, and that smile," he thought. "She's so beautiful."

Cutting up some potatoes, he continued to think of her. Dinner tonight was fried chicken, mashed potatoes, green beans, and dinner rolls.

"I wonder if she'll be out at Grampa's tomorrow?" At that moment, he heard a car screeching in front of the house. Without hesitation, he dropped the knife and potato as he ran out the front door.

The first thing he saw was an old, green Ford stopped in front of the house, in the street. The driver, a man, was getting out. The neighbors from across the street were running towards the car. He looked down and saw Tara sitting in the dirt, rocking back and forth. "Where's Tanya?" he screamed. She didn't answer. She didn't have too. The neighbors were standing around something on the side of the road. Mrs. Johnson was hysterical. Mr. Johnson grabbed her. He pulled her away. Looking over at Little Jack sadly, he shook his head from side to side.

"Call an ambulance!" Mr. Foster yelled.

"Mama," Little Jack whispered, terrified. He turned around and ran into the house. He ran down the hall yelling, "Mama! Mama!" He entered her room as she was waking. He could smell the alcohol but paid it no mind. "Mama!" he yelled again.

"What is it?" she asked. By the tone of her voice, Jack could tell she knew something was wrong. Little Jack didn't act like this.

"Outside," he said before running back that way.

Denise followed him. When she reached the front porch, her heart sank. Tara was in shock. She could tell that at first glance. The car didn't belong on the road like that. She knew what had happened.

"Tanya!" she screamed. She was close behind Little Jack, who was almost to the road. "Tanya!" she screamed again.

Little Jack stopped in horror. Denise kept going. Mr. Foster tried to stop her but was no match. She shoved him clean out of the way. "Tanya!" she screamed for the last time.

Tanya's mangled body lay half in the ditch, half in the road. She was twisted around. Her bottom half was face down in the ditch. Her top half was face up in the road. Little Jack began to weep. Blood was pouring from her mouth, ears and one eye socket. The eye was missing from the socket that was bleeding. "Oh God," Little Jack thought. "Her teeth are on the ground." He could see them.

"No!" Denise cried out at the top of her lungs. Tears flowing, she acted as if she wanted to grab her dead daughter.

The ambulance pulled up at that moment along with the police. The driver of the car, shaking, eyes full of tears himself, began to approach them.

Denise looked at Little Jack. "What did you do?" she asked through grief and tears.

"Nothin' Mama," Little Jack cried back.

"Denise," Mr. Foster said, amazed at her question, but afraid to get too close.

She ignored her older neighbor. "What did you do?" she asked again, walking over to her distraught son.

"I didn't do nothing Mama," Little Jack cried, shaking his head.

The police and ambulance workers were walking toward the scene.

"WHAT DID YOU DO!" Denise screamed full of rage. She delivered a hard and vicious smack to her son's left cheek. The sound of the smack could be heard far away.

"Nothin' Mama!" Little Jack screamed, tears pouring down his face.

Denise grabbed Little Jack by the shoulders. Shaking him back and forth hard, she screamed again, "WHAT DID YOU DO!" Spittle flew from her mouth onto Little Jack's face.

"Enough!" Mr. Foster screamed as he pulled Denise away. She stumbled back. A police officer tried to catch her as she fell but missed. She fell on top of Tanya, mainly on her stomach. The pressure from the fall caused a shower of blood to burst into the air, coming from somewhere deep inside the fallen angel. The sound that escaped made everyone shudder.

"No!" Denise cried as she got off her daughter. She cradled Tanya's head as she sobbed.

"Are you alright?" one of the policemen asked Little Jack.

He ignored the cop and walked towards his mother, crying. "Mama," he mumbled through tears. All the neighbors were crying too.

"Get a way!" She screamed at him while holding Tanya's head, rocking her back and forth, she cried more softly. "Get away."

Embarrassed, and with his heart torn in two, Little Jack looked around at everyone. Everything was spinning. He cried hysterically as the ambulance workers moved in, trying to get Denise away from Tanya. Needing to get their jobs done.

"Jack," a cop said.

Little Jack ignored them all and walked over to Tara, who was still rocking, back and forth on the ground. He embraced his sister and rocked with her, him crying, her lost somewhere far from where they were.

Jack took a deep breath. "Oh, the chicken!" he said, getting up and running into the house. The kitchen was full of smoke. He maneuvered his way around the kitchen and took the frying pan off the heat. The chicken was burnt.

He walked back outside just in time to see one of the ambulance drivers walking off with Tara in his arms. He had wrapped her tightly in a green blanket.

"Tanya," he cried softly as he watched Tara disappear.

LITTLE JACK, TO THIS day, doesn't remember how he got to the hospital, but he made it there. The hours ticked away, with him just sitting in the waiting room.

Some nurses had come to check on him, bringing with them some hot chocolate. He didn't touch it, only asked about Tara and his mother. They told him that Tara was in shock and his mother was with her.

"Jack." Little Jack turned in time to see his grandfather walking toward him, cane in hand.

"Grampa," he said. Standing up, the tears that had disappeared began to rise again. Jack fought it. He didn't want his grandfather to see him cry. Never that.

Grampa gave Jack a long hug when they met in the middle of the hall. "I heard," he said. He hated the smell of hospitals. They reminded him of the war when his knee was blown to hell. They reminded him of his lost wife. One thing was for sure, there were no good memories for him here.

"Tanya," Little Jack said, looking at the floor.

"Are you, Mr. Sampson?" a female voice echoed down the hall. She was a plump lady with a briefcase. She seemed to be about forty-five, but what stuck out the most on her was the hairy mole on the left side of her chin. A little disgusting growth that made Little Jack not even want to look. He didn't like her from jump street.

"I'm Mr. Sampson," Grampa claimed.

"I'm Ruth Stevens. I'm the one who called you. And you must be Jack." She looked at Little Jack, smiling.

Her teeth were crooked and yellow. Jack didn't answer. He looked back to the floor.

"Child services, right?" Grampa said. He said it like he had a bad taste in his mouth. Little Jack caught on right away. He remembered the negative attitude that he had towards these people. At once, he became worried.

"That's right, sir. Could we talk in private?" Miss Stevens continued with that damn smile again.

"Sure," Grampa told her. And to Jack, he said. "I'll be back Jack. Just stay here."

"Are they going to take me away?"

Grampa saw that the boy had a deer caught in the headlights look. It touched his heart in a sad way. "No son, you don't have to worry about that."

Little Jack felt better hearing his grandfather's words until the lady gave him a look that told him otherwise.

Jack sat uncomfortably. A few minutes passed before Grampa came back. He looked upset. "She wants to ask you some questions, Jack. Did your Mama smack you today?"

"I got the black eye from a fight. I don't remember if Mama smacked me." He lied about remembering to be smacked. He remembered it all. It wasn't Mama's fault.

"Well, some of the neighbors, and the police say that she did. We might have some problems."

"What do you mean?"

"They think your Mama may be unfit to take care of you and your sister."

"They don't know what they are talking about."

"I know. I know son. If worse comes to worse, I'll take you two in until this thing blows over."

"I don't want to talk to her, Grampa," Little Jack said, close to panicking.

"It'll be alright Jack. She just wants to make sure you're okay."

The lady, Miss Stevens, smelled like cigarette smoke to Jack. She was sitting at a table across from him, smiling. He had a substitute teacher one time that smelled like that. Gross. "I hope she doesn't ask for a hug when she gets done," he thought.

The questions weren't bad at first. When she asked about Tanya, a lot of things came to his mind, but he blocked out what he remembered and acted as if he forgot everything. The rest of the interview was frustrating for Ruth and uncomfortable for Jack.

"How did it go?" Grampa asked Ruth when they came back to the waiting room. He put his hand on Little Jack's shoulder while waiting for her to answer.

"Well, Mr. Sampson, I'm going to make a call to my supervisor. I've already talked to Denise, the neighbors, and the police. Please wait here."

When she walked away, Grampa knew there was going to be trouble.

"What is she going to do?" Jack asked, still fighting back tears.

"I don't know son." Grampa answered. "I just don't know."

RUTH STEVENS MADE UP her mind at the scene. In her eyes, a drunk mother was asleep and one of the daughters had gotten killed by a car. She then went and physically abused her son. There were witnesses to that. The grandfather had offered to take the children but was sixty-seven years old. He lived in part of a house that was connected to a bar and grill. Not a place for children.

No, the agency was going to have to take the children into custody. When her supervisor agreed, she called the police in case there was a scene. One night is all she was going to allow. Just enough time for the little girl to be released. The police would be there when the time came.

"Mr. Sampson, you can take the boy home with you tonight, if you'll bring him back in the morning."

"No problem, ma'am," Grampa said, a little relieved.

Ruth Stevens turned to Jack. "Jack," she said. "Get a good night's sleep and I'll see you up here tomorrow. Hopefully, your sister will be up and at 'em by then."

"Can I say goodnight to Mama?" Jack asked.

"I don't think that will be a good idea, Jack. She's asleep. You'll see her tomorrow."

Jack concentrated on the hairs growing out of her face as she talked. He wanted to see his mother badly before he left. Wanted to know if she was still angry with him. He'd just have to wait.

"Come on son," Grampa said.

Grampa and Jack left the hospital that night, not knowing the treachery that awaited them the next day.

THAT NIGHT, BACK AT Grampa's house, Little Jack didn't sleep very well at all. He had dreams about Tanya, nightmares. In them, he would walk on the porch to tell the girls that dinner was ready. Tara would get up happily and run into the house.

"Tanya," he would say.

Slowly, she would turn towards him. Her head would be down when she faced him. Her long hair covering her face. Jack knew something was wrong. "Tanya?"

Flipping her hair back with a flash, it would disappear behind her. Her battered face coming into view. One eye was gone, blood flowing out of that socket. Her mouth and ears bleeding as if her head was some type of cryptic fountain. The one good eye, bloodshot, would be looking at Jack. "LOOK AT WHAT YOU DID!" she would scream, blood spraying from a toothless mouth.

Jack woke with a scream, sweating and shivering. Sitting up in bed, he looked at the clock to see that it was five thirty in the morning. There would be no attempts at sleep anytime soon.

At the hospital, Ruth Stevens was already there when the police arrived. She addressed them. "The doctor has released the girl to us. When the boy gets here, we will be prepared to take him. We need you here in case of problems. Here is the court order." Ruth handed the officers the paperwork. One of them looked them over while the other looked around nervously. He hated this part of the job the most.

"Ms. Stevens?"

"Yes," she said, turning around. Another man had joined them. When she saw him, she smiled, "Mr. Phillips, good to see you."

"The office sent me to help."

"Good. Good."

"We've found two homes for them."

"So, it's going to be a split."

"I'm afraid so, we don't have a choice."

"What?" the officer that hadn't looked at the paperwork asked.

Mr. Phillips went on. "The little girl will be staying only one town over at a home for traumatized girls. The lady that runs the home is a licensed child psychologist."

"And the boy?" the officer asked. He had stepped into the conversation and didn't care what they thought.

Ruth looked at him, annoyed. She didn't like the intrusion. This was the only life she had. She didn't have any friends or family. That's why she secretly enjoyed ruining other peoples. "Yes, Mr. Phillips, what about the boy?" she asked with a breath of arrogance.

"He will be going to a home in Chicago."

"Is there a psychologist that lives there?" This was the officer again.

"No," Phillips answered.

"What? You people don't think the boy was traumatized by all of this?"

"Honestly, we don't," Ruth answered. She was truly annoyed by his intrusion.

"Here comes the boy," said the officer with the paperwork. He was just there to do his job.

Grampa and Little Jack had made it to the hospital. Little Jack was very tired. Grampa didn't get much sleep either. No nightmares like Little Jack, but a lot of tossing and turning.

"I'm going to get Mrs. Sampson," Ruth said before letting the grandfather and grandson get to the group.

Grampa and Jack didn't like the look of the police officers standing there. "Why are the police here?" Jack asked.

"Probably just have some questions, could be trouble though," Grampa answered. Little Jack could tell his grandfather was worried, so he gave up on the questioning. Grampa didn't know any more than he did.

When Grampa and Little Jack joined the group, Ruth was coming out of the room followed by Denise.

"Mama," Little Jack said. He was afraid that she would start screaming at him at first. He was relieved to see that she wasn't. She started to cry.

"Jack," she said, dropping to her knees, embracing him in a hug.

They both cried. Denise apologized the whole time. Jack was a little ashamed because he knew Grampa was watching. "It's okay," Little Jack said.

The rest of the group just looked around and waited for the reunion to settle down.

One officer looked at the other and said, "I wonder if that shiner is from the smack."

"No, he got into a fight after school," Grampa Jack answered.

"Yes, the neighbors said he had a black eye before he was assaulted by his mother," Ruth cut in saying.

The officer with the paperwork coughed and said, "Mrs. Sampson. "

She looked from Little Jack to the officer with bloodshot, tear-filled eyes. "Yes."

He tasted coffee as he coughed and said, "I have some papers here from the court."

"Yes," she said again, this time standing up.

"It places the custody of Tara and Jack into the hands of child services."

"What do you mean?" she asked in shock. She knew but didn't want it to be true.

"We've got to take them from you," he said in an authoritative voice.

Grampa Jack looked at Ruth and asked, "Can't they stay with me until things get better?"

"Our supervisors don't think it would be a good idea."

"Well, you must have given me a bad report then, lady," Grampa's voice was rising.

Denise broke in. "No one is taking my children."

"Mrs. Sampson," Mr. Phillips said. "I'm afraid you don't have a choice."

"Watch your mouth, you silly bastard," Grampa said. "Who the hell are you anyway?"

"I'm with family services," Phillips answered, a little frightened.

"Mr. Sampson," Ruth Stevens said.

"Lady, you better shut up before I slap that hairy wart off your face," Grampa said, pulling off his overcoat, readying himself for battle.

Ruth Stevens grabbed the hairy mole, shocked. It was as if she was picturing the act.

"Calm down, Jack," the officer that didn't want to be there said, trying to defuse the situation.

"You're not taking my children," Denise said, hysterically.

"We have to," Ruth said. "It may only be temporary."

Little Jack had to stand up and agree to go before they would all settle down. He didn't want to see his grandfather and mother fight with the police like his father did. They might end up in prison.

Ruth and the man called Phillips had the officers make Grampa and Denise leave. "I'm going to talk to a judge," Grampa had said before leaving.

"We'll be leaving after the doctor sees Tara," Ruth said to Little Jack with that smile and awful breath.

Little Jack sat in a chair staring at the floor, waiting. He'd been doing a lot of that lately.

Chapter 7

The politeness that Ruth and Phillips had shown Little Jack disappeared with Mama, Grampa, and the police.

"Where am I going?" Jack had asked when the others left.

"Just have a seat over there," Ruth said, pointing to a chair in the waiting room.

Jack had obeyed. He sat very nervously while the two child service workers talked. He didn't pay attention to their words but could tell that Ruth was impressed by Mr. Phillips. Carl, he had told her to call him.

Carl Phillips was half of a foot taller than Ruth. He was balding and wore glasses. He wore a mustache that he kept neat and trimmed. His suit was gray and cheap along with his shoes.

An overweight nurse came out of Tara's room. "She's ready when you are."

Jack's heart dropped when he heard. The butterflies came to his stomach. He felt as if he might be sick.

The nurse left as quickly as she had appeared.

Ruth turned to Jack and said, "Come on."

The trio went to Tara's room. When the little girl saw Jack, her eyes lit up. "Jack," she said excitedly. Jumping off her bed, she ran to him with open arms. Jack embraced his sister. Fighting back tears, he squeezed.

"Okay," Ruth said. "We'll be leaving now."

Tara looked at Ruth and Mr. Carl Phillips. She then looked at Jack. "We have to go with them." She said she didn't ask.

"I know," Little Jack said. "It will be alright. It'll only be for a little while. Mama and Grampa Jack are on their way to talk to a judge."

"Let's go," Carl said. They left the hospital.

Denise had told Tara before she left that her and Jack would be going with Ruth for a while.

"Are they going to babysit us?" Tara had asked.

"For a while sweetie," Denise answered.

Tara had no idea what was in store for them.

Out in the parking lot, the four walked to two different cars. "Jack, you ride with me, and Tara will ride with Ruth," Carl said before opening the door on his brown Plymouth.

"Why?" Jack asked.

"Because I said," Carl retorted angrily. "Now get in the damn car."

"Listen to Mr. Phillips," Ruth said.

"Where are we going?" Jack asked. He looked over at Tara and realized she was about to cry.

"We are going to your new home. It will only be for a while. Now you have a choice, we can do this the easy way or the hard way. Look at your poor sister over there. You've done made her cry again," Carl said. Jack looked at Tara again. "Alright," he said.

"Get in Tara," Ruth ordered.

"Okay," Tara said, climbing in.

Jack climbed in with Carl. Both cars drove off to the edge of the parking lot. Ruth and Tara in front with Jack and Carl behind.

"How long are we going to stay at this place?" Tara asked Ruth while they were waiting on the traffic to clear. It was thick and congested with automobiles.

"What do you mean, we?" Ruth asked. She then looked at the frightened little girl evilly and said, "You're going far away from your brother and mother. You might not ever see them again."

"No!" Tara screamed. The tears flowing. She tried to exit the vehicle on her side.

"Sit still," Ruth said as she pulled Tara with one hand, driving out of the lot.

Jack, from the car behind, saw Tara struggle. "What is she doing?" he asked, watching Ruth with her hawk-like grip on his sister pull out.

"I don't know," Carl answered waiting to drive away himself.

"She better not hurt her," Jack said, on the verge of snapping.

"Or what, you ungrateful little punk?" Carl said, pulling out into the road.

"You're going the wrong way," Jack cried out, looking back in the direction that his sister was going.

"Listen Jack, you need to calm down and listen to what I have to say."

"What?"

"You and your sister aren't going to the same place."

"What?"

"You heard me."

Jack couldn't breathe but managed to say, "You can't do that."

"We can do what we want Jack. We work for the state, and you are a ward of the state now."

"What about the funeral?" Jack asked. Tears had begun to fall down his cheeks, but he wasn't crying just tears.

"That's up to the Judge, son."

"Don't call me son," Little Jack said.

"A tough, little smart ass, huh? You little punk," Carl said. He then punched Little Jack as hard as he could, knocking him unconscious.

Little Jack didn't know how long he had been out. He did know that he had been dreaming. The dream was of Tanya again, but this time she was looking peaceful in her coffin. They must have been at her funeral. He woke slowly, scared at first to open his eyes. Not knowing what to expect. The purr of the engine brought everything back to him too quickly. He looked to his left and saw Carl driving. Looking out the window, he saw that he had entered the big city of Chicago.

Carl Phillips looked over to see Little Jack looking at him, "I don't know why the state wastes its time and money for people like you."

Little Jack began to cry. Tears of anger, not sadness.

"I mean, look at you. Your little black eye shows that you aren't that tough."

Little Jack suddenly had that look he had when it was time to fight.

Carl kept going. "Oh, look at the tears on the tough guy."

"Whop!" Little Jack gave Carl Phillips a left jab.

The shot dazed the man, causing him to swerve the car. They were on a busy street. To avoid a collision, Carl had to swerve the car back to the other side. He side-swiped a parked car.

"Crack!" Little Jack landed a right.

"Stop!" Carl screamed. He slammed on the brakes. Little Jack wasn't ready for this. His head smashed into the windshield. His ribs hit the dashboard. The windshield shattered. Little Jack's head began to bleed. He was dazed but shook it off at about the same time Carl Phillips was shaking off the surprisingly hard punches he had just received from a twelve-year-old boy.

Little Jack got out of the car and looked around. He only knew that he was in Chicago, but not where in Chicago.

"Punk," Carl said as he grabbed onto Little Jack's shirt. Jack hadn't even heard the man get out of the car.

Little Jack instinctively kicked Carl in the shin. Carl let go with a yelp. Little Jack, out of the man's grasp, stood back and took a stance.

"I got a ten on the kid," a man yelled to the right.

Little Jack looked around and saw that a crowd had gathered. He wasn't worried about them. He'd had enough. "Come on," he told Carl Phillips through clenched teeth and with a wave of his hand. The hand wave clearly meaning bring it on.

The crowd erupted into a cheer. At the sound of that, Carl looked worried. "I am a state worker. This boy is a delinquent in my custody."

"We don't care in this neighborhood, Mister," a man shouted from the crowd.

"You people caused enough problems here already," a lady said.

"Clock!" Little Jack stumbled the man with a quick left. Carl steadied himself, ready to fight. He took a step forward and swung. Little Jack ducked and was out of the way quick. He brought up a right upper cut with all he had. Carl stumbled back and hit one knee. Little Jack followed the grown man's movements serving him a right, left combination. Carl Phillips hit the ground unconscious.

As Little Jack listened to the crowd cheer Mr. Phillips defeat, he also heard sirens. He saw a police car approaching fast. Startled, he ran through the crowd. He ran as fast as he could. He didn't have to know the city to know how to get away from the police. "Man, I'm in trouble," he thought as he turned down an alley. At the end of the alley, he quickly jumped into a dumpster. It reminded him of the one out at the back of the jail back home.

BACK AT THE SCENE THERE was total chaos. The Police pulled up to see a kid finishing off a grown man in a fistfight next to a crashed, brown Plymouth. A crowd of the neighborhood people were on the curb, cheering loudly.

After questioning the crowd, the police ended up with only three women who were willing to talk. They all had the same story. The car had crashed, and a boy had got out bleeding. The man grabbed him, so they started fighting. The boy won.

The police called an ambulance and a juvenile detective down at the station.

When awakened, an embarrassed Carl Phillips had another story. He said that he was driving when the boy, out of nowhere, assaulted him, causing the crash. He said that when he got out of the car, the boy had used a weapon, a pipe that he'd picked up off the ground.

Detective Paul Donovan entered the scene as it was clearing. After hearing the facts, he walked over to Carl Phillips. "Looks like one of them finally let you have it, Carl."

"This kid is a menace, "Carl said. He was sitting in the back of the ambulance with his feet on the ground. He had a cloth held over the left side of his face. The swollen side.

Donovan figured he had the real cause of all this drama right here in his sight. He'd had numerous complaints about Carl Phillips back before he transferred to the central district. "In your statement that you gave the other officers, you said that the boy used a weapon."

"Yes, he did."

"Well, that's funny Carl," Donovan said with a chuckle as he tried to look into the other man's eyes.

"What's funny about that?" Carl asked, keeping his eyes focused on his cheap shoes.

"What's funny about it is when the officers pulled up, they saw the end of the scuffle and they didn't see the boy strike you with any weapon."

"Well, maybe he got rid of it before then."

"Well maybe he did, and I thought about that Carl, but that wouldn't match the statements of the witnesses who saw the whole thing go down. Do you care to recant your statement?"

"No," Carl said without raising his head.

"Just to let you know Carl," Donovan said before leaving. "I'll be at the hearing tomorrow before Judge Bodell."

Carl Phillips didn't like hearing that but didn't say anything. He just wanted the cop to leave.

BACK AT THE DUMPSTER, Little Jack's breathing returned to normal. The blood had stopped flowing from the cut on his head and he had stopped shaking. It was around that time that the smell of the dumpster became too much for him. Lifting his head and the lid up he didn't see any police. He thought this would be an enjoyable time as any to high tail it out of there before they all decided to show up. Mr. Phillips did say that he was a state worker.

"I guess he's like a cop," Little Jack said to himself. He climbed out of the dumpster and made it halfway down the alley before he heard someone.

"You're the kid from the fight, aren't ya?"

Little Jack turned around to see a kid a little older than him, looking at him smiling. The boy had on a nice gray shirt that stuck out to Little Jack. He had on a gold necklace and gold watch. His eyes were blue like Little Jack's and his hair was light. Not sandy brown like his, but almost white. Besides his hair being lighter they could have passed for brothers.

"What's your name?" the boy asked.

Jack heard the question but didn't answer the boy at first. He studied him further. "He doesn't mean me any trouble," he thought before answering. "They call me, Ace."

"Ace huh?" the boy said, looking him up and down. "Well Ace, they call me CJ."

"What does CJ stand for?" Jack asked.

"Christopher Joseph, but don't tell anybody."

"Okay," Little Jack agreed.

"Let's go," said CJ as he started to walk away.

"Where to?"

"Ace, we got to get you out of here. They just cleared the scene, but there's still some cops down there. You'll be safe with me...Come on."

"Sure," Little Jack said. He could use all the help he could get.

"Don't worry," CJ said as he led Little Jack away. "My dad runs this neighborhood."

Chapter 8

Denise and Grampa Jack couldn't get in to see a judge that day, but the next morning was a different story. Grampa Jack had made sure his lawyer was there first thing in the morning.

"Little Jack ran off," the lawyer said before the hearing. He was fiftyish with salt and pepper hair, in decent shape and dressed nicely. He took all his cases seriously. He had hawk-like features that a lot of women found attractive. He was faithful to his wife and loved his children so the looks and passes that were sometimes made to him were a waste of time. His days of living the bachelor lifestyle were long gone.

"What do you mean he ran off?" Denise cried. The tears began to pour like they had so many times during the last few days.

"What's going on?" Grampa jumped in; His voice was incredibly angry.

"I'm sure he'll be alright," the lawyer said, reassuringly. "We'll get all the details at the hearing. A detective from the juvenile division is coming in all the way from Chicago."

"Why Chicago?" Denise asked. The tears had stopped but hearing the word Chicago made the worrying multiply.

"Mama," all heads turned at the sound of Tara. She ran to her mother and gave her a fierce hug.

The tears began to fall again, down the face of Denise Sampson. "It's okay baby," she cried. "Everything is okay."

Ruth and Carl stood close by but felt awkward. Carl sported a nice shiner from the day before. Ruth was watching Tara closely. She had threatened the little girl before they got there, telling her that if she talked to her mother or anyone about the day before she would get the police and have them take her to jail. Tara was truly terrified. Ruth always mentally tortured the younger children. And after a few threats, she never had anything to worry about.

Tara saw Ruth eyeballing her and squeezed harder. She wasn't going to tell.

"What happened to Jack," Grampa asked, looking at Carl.

"It will all come out at the hearing," Carl said. His sour attitude shining through.

"Ha," Grampa laughed, "he blacked your eye, didn't he...Punk?"

"Mr. Donovan," the lawyer, Roger Peters, cut in saying before Carl could answer.

"Roger, how are you?" Paul Donovan said, walking to the group. Everyone except Tara turned to see the big man. She kept a tight grip on Denise. Carl only looked for a second. He didn't want to be there.

"Ready for you," a bailiff said behind the group.

They all went into Judge Bodell's courtroom.

Everything had come out at the hearing except for what Ruth had done to Tara.

Ruth started out giving her report of the events that led up to then. In her final summation, she requested that the children be kept by the state.

Denise explained to the judge that she had taken a nap when Tanya died and that the children always played outside without any problems. When asked about smacking Jack, she cried even harder and said she was out of her head when it happened.

Grampa testified that Jack was happy with his home life and that his daughter in law was a fine mother, a single mother of three at that. He sounded convincing. One would think that him and Judge Bodell went back a long way.

Carl Phillips told his side of the story about the day before. He acted like he had been nice to the boy when suddenly, he attacked for no reason.

Paul Donovan told a different story. A tale of former complaints of abuse. He said that the on-scene officers didn't see any weapons, none were found at the scene, and that the citizen witnesses all had the same story. He went on to explain to the judge that the boy had exited the vehicle, bleeding from the head. Denise began to sob at this. Donovan paused for effect then went on to say that the witnesses saw Mr. Phillips grab Jack and they exchanged blows. The boy ran when he heard the police arrive at the scene.

Grampa Jack couldn't help but smile at Carl who again looked at the ground.

Next to testify was the child psychologist who had received Tara the day before. She gave a good report on Tara's mind and to the surprise of Ruth and Carl said she didn't see any problem with the little girl going home.

Tara had been out in the hallway during all of this. It being decided by Judge Bodell before the hearing. The old bailiff had been excused to watch her and keep her company. He was happy because to him nothing was more boring than a custody hearing.

"I'm calling for a recess until eleven 'o clock," Judge Bodell said at ten thirty. The hearing had gone on for an hour and a half. Those who knew the honorable Judge Bodell closely knew that his prostate didn't allow him to sit anywhere for very much longer than that.

"What do you think?" Peters asked Paul Donovan. They were standing with Grampa. Denise had Tara on her lap on a bench nearby.

"I've never dealt with Bodell personally," Donovan said, "But his reputation as a fair and hard judge stretches throughout all of Illinois."

"I can't tell either," Peters said, looking at his client, Grampa Jack.

"Don't worry about it, son," Grampa said, confidently.

"I think the children should be at home with their mother," Donovan said.

Grampa Jack nodded his head in approval at the officer. Then asked. "What's being done to find Jack?"

"I spent last night asking all around the neighborhood about him where all of this went down. People are reluctant to talk to me about anything. It's an Irish neighborhood. I want to get a photo of him to show to the officers that have that beat."

"I can get you one," Grampa said.

"He probably thinks he's in big trouble," Peters said.

"Yeah," said Donovan. "He probably doesn't want to be found by the police."

"It's a long way from here," Grampa said.

"I wouldn't worry too much," Peters said. "He's a tough kid."

"He's ready for you," The bailiff said behind them.

"I'll be back, sweetie," Denise told Tara.

The group made their way back inside. All members of the previous party sat in the same seats as earlier. A couple of minutes passed before the court clerk announced Judge Bodell. All rose.

"Be seated," Judge Bodell said to the respectfully standing group.

"I'm ready to rule in this hearing," he began. "I've been sitting on this bench for almost twenty years. Each of these cases is unique in their own ways. The way I see the events are, the mother took out her anguish on her son at the sight of her dead child," he paused briefly. "What I had to ask myself was this; Does this make her a bad mother? No, it doesn't. As far as the boy goes, there are more witnesses with different stories than Mr. Phillips. This is the bottom line, Mr. Phillips, working for the state, took Jack Sampson for his own protection, and in the process lost him. The last sight of the boy was him running into a strange neighborhood, bleeding from the head." Bodell's voice was raised in anger.

Denise started to cry again.

"It is the decision of this court to place the custody of the children back with their mother."

Peters put his arm around Denise. She cried harder into his shoulder.

Bodell went on. "Of course, we'll have to wait to find the boy before we can get him home where he belongs."

A profound sense of relief washed over Grampa, Denise, Peters, and Donovan.

"Mrs. Sampson," Judge Bodell said. "Put this behind you as much as you can and go bury your daughter."

"Thank you, your Honor," Denise cried.

Paul Donovan reassured Grampa and Denise that he would devote as much time as he could to finding Little Jack and getting him back home.

AT THE FUNERAL THE next day, all were sad in attendance. Still no word had come down about the whereabouts of Little Jack.

The parlor was jam packed. The tragedy had affected everyone in the community. To come and pay their last respects was a must for all. Denise apologized to the neighbors that witnessed her outburst and horrible treatment of her son. They all told her she wasn't in her head at the time. Everyone cried together.

Tanya Sampson, laid out in a white dress, looked like an angel. Her beautiful blond hair cascaded down her body. Her closed eyes and relaxed face made her look as at peace as one could be under the circumstances. Everyone thought the mortician had done a wonderful job.

Grampa Jack gave the eulogy. Afterward, when Amazing Grace began to play, the people began to pay their last respects to Tanya Sampson.

Everyone watched in tears as Tara made her way to the casket. The little girl placed a rose in with her sister as she cried fountains of sad tears. She kissed Tanya on the forehead and whispered something no one could hear. She walked two steps from her identical twin sister before she lunged back and latched on to her. "Tanya!" she screamed. She was hysterical, crying out. "No! Tanya! No!"

Denise was there fast. She took her daughter and picked her up. Tara put her arms around her mother, wrapping her legs around her waist as she cried into her chest, great heaving sobs. Denise handed Tara off to Mrs. Johnson. Tara latched on in the same manner, her crying never relaxing.

Denise then walked down, crying as she said goodbye to her daughter.

Tanya Sampson was buried that day with all her loved ones in attendance, except her brother, Jack.

Cindy Thompson was there and sick with grief like the rest. She had ridden to the funeral with Grampa Jack. It was hard to tell the little girl that morning about Little Jack still being lost in the city. He knew that they had a special bond.

"Did you eat breakfast?" Grampa had asked.

She just looked at the floor. Truth be told, she hadn't eaten dinner the night before either. She had been too upset to do anything when she found out what had happened to Jack and Tanya. Tanya dying was hard on her, but this was too much in such a brief time.

"Sit down," Grampa told her. "I've got to fix breakfast before we go."

He noticed that Cindy had her hair pulled back with her church dress on. "Did you tell your Mama where you were going?"

"She didn't come home last night," Cindy answered. The smell of the bacon made her stomach growl. The need for food temporarily overpowered her grief.

Grampa was furious when he heard this but tried his hardest not to let it show. "You know Cindy, I could use a waitress here in the afternoons."

"Really," Cindy said, lighting up.

"Yes, and I already talked to my waitress, Julie. She agreed that she could use some help in here serving dinner to all these customers."

"I can do it."

"Well, since she's the head waitress, you'll only get a percentage of the tips. I'll be paying you by the hour anyway. And of course, you'll get a free dinner every night. As much as you can eat."

"Okay, Grampa Jack."

The old man smiled at being called Grampa by such a sweet little girl. "Eat up," he said. At this point, they both registered where they were about to go and what was happening that day. Sadness came over them both.

After the funeral, people piled into 'Jack's Bar and Grill.' Cindy began her job and was a natural. Julie showed her the ropes as the little girl flew along. She was so busy that she forgot her grief for the time being.

Grampa Jack was happy to see the little girl getting along so good. He gave her the job to keep an eye on her and make sure she got a decent meal in her at night. All the patrons tipped more generously and even after giving Cindy her cut, Julie realized she was making more than usual.

Part of the deal was that Cindy would go to school every day and keep her grades up. The change was good for her.

Chapter 9

CJ had treated Little Jack good the night before. After maneuvering through a couple of yards and alleys, Little Jack found himself standing on the outside of a tall wooden fence. The noise inside was familiar to the young scrapper's ears. There was a fight going on inside.

"Come on," CJ said, making his way from the alley along the side of the fence. When CJ entered the yard, Little Jack followed his new friend without hesitation.

The yard was big and lighted. People were crowded around the action. Some on top of two old cars, others on barrels. Most of the men were on the ground. CJ led Little Jack to a spigot. "Clean up all that blood," he told him.

Little Jack did just that. As he washed off the dried-up blood, he realized it wasn't people that were fighting. It was dogs.

"Up here," CJ said disappearing up an antenna and climbing onto the top of an old truck that Little Jack hadn't noticed before because of the crowd. Little Jack followed his new friend to get a better look at the action.

"Wow," he said once up top. They all surrounded a pit dug in the middle of the yard. Two pit bulls were battling viciously. One was solid black with a white patch on its throat. The other was solid white with pink eyes.

Little Jack estimated that there were about thirty men screaming around the pit, cheering on the dog that they had put their hard-earned cash on. Some of them with that cash in their hands.

"The white one is my father's, "CJ yelled to Jack. "GO PINKY GO!"

"GO PINKY!" Jack screamed, engulfed by the action.

The two dogs took turns biting each other, neither one being able to land a throat shot for a while. Little Jack could smell the excitement and blood. His heart raced as sweat began to pour out of his forehead.

Finally, Pinky hit his mark. The black dog didn't have a chance after that. Pinky shook back and forth. Growling and clamping down, Pinky was slowly taking the life of the other dog. The men seemed to settle down when they saw this. Some of them cursed, obviously the ones who chose the wrong dog.

Little Jack settled down himself and began to feel a little panicked. Were they going to let the dog die? The black dog had given up all attempts to fight back.

Finally, Little Jack saw a big man with a gold chain, gold watch, and a gold pinky ring looking at a man across the pit from him. The man on the other side of the pit nodded to the big man. The big man nodded to another man, who went in and broke the dogs up. The defeated dog laid still. Little Jack looked at his friend.

CJ saw the worry on Jack's face. Smiling, he said, "Don't worry, he ain't dead. Probably won't fight again, but he ain't dead."

The men in the yard started paying each other off. "Tomorrow," the big man with all the gold said. The men started to leave.

"That's my father," CJ said proudly.

Little Jack witnessed the first man that CJ's father had nodded to go and pick up the black dog. "Maybe next time, huh Jimbo?" The first man said with a pat on the losing man's back.

"Tomorrow," the other man said with a smile. Little Jack was surprised to see there wasn't any anger in the man that was holding his hurt dog. If there was, he didn't show it.

"Anything else?" It was the man who had broken up the fight and ran Pinky into a building.

"Nothing Tom," CJ's father said, handing him a few bills off a roll from his pocket. "Tomorrow."

"I'll be here, Rick," Tom said before disappearing.

"What's up Pops?" CJ said to his father.

"Another day, another dollar," Rick said, looking at his son with a smile. Little Jack could tell that they were father and son. No doubt about it. CJ was just a smaller version of the big man. Same light hair, same blue eyes, and the same smile.

"Who's your friend?" he asked after taking notice of the other boy with the black eye and cut on his head. He looked as if he'd been through a lot in a short period of time.

"This is Ace, Pops. From the fight down the street earlier. Did you hear about it?"

"Yes," Rick said, looking Little Jack over in a different light. "Did you whoop a state worker?"

Little Jack nodded at Rick without smiling.

It's alright," CJ said. "My pops knows everything that happens in this neighborhood."

"Rick O'Reilly," Rick said, outstretching his hand to the lad.

"Ace Sampson," Little Jack said, taking his friend's father's hand and shaking it.

"You don't say," Rick said, looking at the boy strangely. "I was in prison with a guy named Ace Sampson. He was a boxer."

Little Jack was shocked at hearing this. The look on his face confirmed what the man knew. Rick saw the resemblance when he heard the name. "He was my father," Little Jack said.

No wonder you whooped a grown man, son. Your father was the best fighter I ever seen. It's a shame what happened. I got out before then, but when I was there, I made a lot of money bettin' on your old man."

Little Jack didn't say anything, just nodded and smiled proudly.

"The cops are trying to find him Pops, we got to look out for him."

"Sure, no problem," Rick said without hesitation. "CJ sleeps outside this time of year, Ace. Is that alright with you?"

"Sure," Little Jack answered. He could think of worse places to have to sleep. He definitely didn't want to go to jail.

As night fell, the boys, full from a good dinner, settled down at their little campsite. They would sleep on a mattress in the back of the truck. CJ had brought out an extra blanket for Jack. "That will keep you warm," CJ said. "It's the same as mine."

Little Jack threw the blanket into the back of the truck. The boys sat on the ground by a small fire, in a little pit, with rocks around it.

"Why do you sleep out here?" Little Jack asked. He wasn't complaining because it was peaceful and beautiful to him. The sky was full of stars. The full moon in view. Sitting around the campfire, Jack couldn't even tell he was in the city. No, he wasn't complaining. He was simply curious.

"Back when Pops was in the joint," CJ began. "It was just me and Mama until she got sick. She had the cancer and didn't last long. Ate her up."

"I'm sorry to hear that."

"No, it's okay. She's better off now."

"Do you think she is in heaven?"

"Yeah," CJ answered. "Anyway, the state people came and took me away. It was a farm, far away from the city. The people there were really mean, Jack."

"What do you mean?"

"The man was always hitting me with something, and they made me work like a slave from before sunrise until after sundown. So, I just ran off. Pops owned this house, so it was just sitting here. I just fended for myself until he got out. I sleep inside in the winter, but during the summer, I'm out here."

"How'd you eat?" Little Jack was amazed at his friend's story.

"Everybody knows Pops around here. The neighbor to the left figured out what was going on. Before long, all the right people knew what to do for me."

"How long was you on your own?"

"Mama died when I was nine. I stayed at the foster home until I was ten. Pops got out of prison when I was twelve. I'm thirteen now, so two years here on my own."

"Your only thirteen?"

"Yeah, I look older, don't I?"

"Yeah, I thought you was fifteen."

THEY SAT IN SILENCE for a while. CJ poked at the fire with a stick. "Why'd the state get ya, Ace?"

Little Jack was caught off guard by the question. He looked at his friend, deciding whether to tell him. It wasn't like he was going to turn him in. So, Little Jack poured out his story. Starting with his father, he took CJ on a ride. He told the story of his sister and ended at the current event today. He was hurt but didn't cry.

"Jesus, Ace," CJ said. He had a tear in his eye but didn't let it fall. His friend had lost his Pops, his sister was freshly dead with the other more or less kidnapped. He was far away from home and wanted by the law, and with a stranger at that. "I'm sorry man."

"Don't be," Little Jack said. They sat in silence for a long time before talking about normal things. Jack looking off, getting lost in the stars, wondering what it was really like up there.

The boys laid under their blankets. The fire had gone out, but they were warm.

"Do you have a girlfriend?" CJ asked.

"Yes."

"What's her name?"

"Cindy," Little Jack answered, still lost in the stars. "Cindy," he thought to himself as he drifted off to sleep.

Chapter 10

Little Jack woke up with the morning sun shining brightly on his face. He didn't know where he was at first, but it came back to him quickly. He was filled with a surge of grief and guilt as he thought of his little sister. "Tanya, poor little Tanya," he thought.

"Mornin' Ace." CJ had walked up to the side of the truck. Little Jack didn't even realize that he wasn't next to him when he had risen from his slumber.

"My head hurts," Little Jack said. Forgetting his grief, he felt the cut. It was a little swollen, but not bad.

"Don't push it too hard," CJ said. "It might make it worse or make it start to bleed again."

"I'm not."

"Here," said CJ, handing Jack two egg sandwiches.

Little Jack eagerly accepted the food saying, "Thanks," before eating half of the first one in a single bite.

"Them should hold you over until lunch. Pops is going to cook out with some friends this afternoon before the fights tonight."

"It's plenty, thank you," Jack said in between bites.

"Well, I got to do my chores," CJ said. "Do you want to help?"

"Sure."

"If you want some water to wash them sandwiches down just use the same spigot over there that you used yesterday to clean up in."

"Thank you," Little Jack said. He got up and jumped down from the truck. CJ waited as his friend refreshed himself and washed up. "Where can I pee?" Little Jack asked when he returned from the spigot.

"Just go over there by the fence," CJ answered, pointing to another part of the yard. "I'll be in the shed when you get done. Knock first and I'll let you in. Don't just walk-in cause I might have one of the dogs out and they don't know you yet."

"Alright," Little Jack answered, running off to relieve himself.

LITTLE JACK WAS AMAZED when he joined his friend in the shed. There were twelve pit bulls in pens. CJ had two more out of their cages running on treadmills. The treadmills were separated by chicken wire with both dogs running in the opposite direction. "I already fed them," CJ said to Little Jack. "Got to water them next."

"What do you want me to do?"

"Well, if you take them buckets out and fill them up, we'll get done quicker."

Little Jack went and did his part. The boys worked hard to get the chores over with. Little Jack liked taking part, working to keep such wonderful dogs in shape. He didn't show fear when handling and getting to know any of them. Looking around after giving each dog its turn on the treadmill and scooping up all the droppings out of the cage, Little Jack was happy that not one of the dogs even growled at him.

"They must like ya," CJ had said.

When they were done, CJ led his friend out of the shed. "I like having you around," he said, smiling at Little Jack. "I ain't never got them dogs done that quick."

"It's the least I could do," Little Jack told his friend as he followed him out of the yard. "Where are we going?"

"Down to the pool hall. Do you play?"

"I've played before at my Grampa's bar."

"I don't play unless it's for cash. Pops said there ain't no other reason to play. He puts money on everything he does. He comes out good too."

"Yeah."

"Yeah, he says it's in our blood. Says some people lose money on everything they touch but not us."

"I've never put much thought into money one way or the other. Never had much use for it." As Little Jack told his friend this, his mind drifted to the fishing poles he had worked hard for the summer before. He blanked the thought out as quickly as it came. He didn't need to be thinking of home just yet. Being a wanted fugitive and all, the police were probably watching the house and bar right now.

THE POOL HALL WAS SMOKEY when the boys entered from the side door. Hank Williams was playing on the juke box. Always something to remind him of home.

"CJ." Little Jack heard a few people say as a greeting.

"What's going on, fellas," CJ said back, walking to an open table.

Little Jack noticed that there were seven pool tables in the place and that CJ had just taken the last open one. There were about thirty teenagers going about their business throughout the building. A couple of kids, about fifteen or sixteen years old, eyed Little Jack suspiciously, but from what he could see, most of them minded their own business and didn't even notice him.

"Rack 'em up," CJ said from his side of the table.

The two friends played a game of pool. Little Jack didn't have a chance. CJ let him have it with no mercy since it was a friendly game, no bet.

"Who wants to play for some scratch?" CJ yelled. A few heads turned, but for the most part, people paid him no mind.

"I got ya," an older fella said from the side door entrance. Little Jack, CJ and some others turned to see him walk in followed by three other fellas and two girls. The boys were about sixteen, their hair slicked back, full of grease. They had leather jackets on top of white t-shirts and denim jeans that stretched to their biker boots. All the boys had cigarettes hanging from their mouths.

The girls were wearing long, pleated, light green skirts and white blouses. Their hair was pulled back with ribbons holding it in place.

"I've got some payback comin', don't ya think?" the obvious leader of the group said to CJ.

"Sure do," CJ said. "Rack 'em up."

Little Jack knew trouble when he saw it and if this wasn't a brawl in the making, he didn't know what was. He looked over to CJ who winked and smiled at him while lifting the chalk up to his stick. Little Jack smiled back and sat down at a nearby table to watch the action.

"You're the boy from the fight," one of the girls said. The three other boys and two girls were at the table next to him. "He's the one I was talking about, Rita," she said to the other girl.

"How old are you?" The girl named Rita asked Little Jack.

"Fifteen," he lied without looking at the girls. He could pass for fifteen. A small fifteen.

"Where's the beer?" one of the boys asked, looking around.

At the far end of the establishment a boy got up from a chair carrying a bucket. He walked over and sold an ice-cold beer to the boy who had asked. From listening to the greasers talk, Little Jack learned that the boy's father owned place but was never there. He didn't want to be there in case the police ever showed up. The son's job was to pass out cold beers for a good profit.

"I want one," the first girl who spoke earlier said. The boy with the bucket, halfway back to his chair stopped and turned around. Walking back through the smokey room, he did his business. It looked to Little Jack that he didn't really want to be there.

"I'm buyin'," one of the boys said.

"Thank you, Todd," the girl said.

"Alright, Todd," another boy said.

"Want a beer, Ace," CJ asked from the pool table. "I'm buyin." Little Jack shook his head. "Well, I believe I'll partake," CJ said as he reached into his wallet to pay for his beer.

About five beers later, Rita and her friends were a lot friendlier. She had joined Little Jack's table and wouldn't shut up. She told him that she was a Kitten, and the boys were The Tigers. Little Jack had to fight not to laugh at hearing this. They were part of a local gang. She said that CJ and the leader, Blade, played pool all the time with CJ usually winning Blade's money. "You're cute," she had whispered before moving back to the table with her friends. Little Jack blushed.

It was a quarter to twelve when CJ said, "Last game."

"What do you mean last game?" Blade asked. He was definitely mad about it.

"Last game man. I got to get home."

"You can't just win all of my money and then quit."

"I'll meet you back here at eight tonight if you want to keep going."

"Son of a bitch," Blade cursed. "If my daddy wasn't so tight with your daddy CJ, I'd whoop you up and down the street."

"Don't be so confident," CJ said. Little Jack stood up at hearing that.

"You don't want any problems with the Tigers," Blade said, putting down his beer on the pool table.

"Are you going to be here tonight or what?" CJ asked, not backing down a bit.

"I'll be here."

"Alright then." CJ said walking out of the joint with Little Jack on his tail.

Back at the house, the back yard was filled with the familiar smell of BBQ.

"You boys are just in time," Rick said when the boys came into view. There were five other guys there. One of them was Tom, the guy who broke up the fight the day before and put Pinky up.

The boys ate their fill and climbed up to the top of the old truck they had slept in the night before.

The yard started to fill up with gamblers. "Beer?" Rick yelled to CJ over the crowd. CJ nodded his head, yes and his father brought him a cold one. "Ace?" the man asked. Little Jack declined the offer.

The yard was alive. The men screaming over their choice of dog in the first fight. Rick's dog eventually won and Little Jack could see that about half of the men had chosen the right dog.

After that first fight, a man in a suit came into the yard followed by a couple of tough looking, burly fellas that were obviously his bodyguards. One of them had a mean looking pit bull on a leash. The dog had a white body and an all-brown head.

CJ took a swallow of his second beer since he got home, while looking at the man in the suit. He then looked at Little Jack and spoke. "That's Tank O' Cannon. He's got some good dogs."

"Looks like a mean one."

"Pops will put Spot up against him. If Pinky wouldn't have fought last night, he'd put him up." That made sense to Little Jack. He and CJ watched as Rick walked over to shake Tank's hand.

"Pops and he go way back. Tank runs the west side of the city. He makes it over here sometimes, I heard him tell Pops, so he can cut loose for a spell. He knows Pop's dogs are tough too."

When the crowd saw Tom come out with Spot, bets were placed immediately. It wasn't long after that that the dogs were going at it. Both desperately trying to snatch on to the other's throat. "Get him, Spot!" Little Jack caught himself screaming along with CJ. They were cheering for the right dog. Spot found his mark and latched on. Little Jack noticed that through the whole fight, Tank O' Cannon didn't get excited. Even now, as he sat and watched his dog dying, his expression didn't change. The crowd began to die down as the inevitable approached.

Rick looked at Tank while waiting for the approving nod. When it came, he looked to Tom, who broke up the fight.

Tank O' Cannon looked at one of his bodyguards. The bodyguard reached into his suitcoat and pulled out a .22 caliber pistol, walked over, and fired two shots into the downed dog's head.

CJ said, "Five bucks," and got up. Little Jack looked over to Tank who was waving CJ over. He jumped off the truck, grabbed a shovel and ran to Tank. Tank reached into his pocket, pulled out a wad of bills, snatched one off the top, and handed it to CJ. He took the money and ran for a wheelbarrow on the other side of the truck. "Come on, and I'll split it with you," CJ told Jack.

"Alright," Jack said. He jumped down and ran over to the dog. CJ pulled up with the wheelbarrow, the shovel on top. Little Jack picked up the dog, making sure not to get any blood on his only pair of clothes. He deposited the dog into the wheelbarrow and the duo left the back yard.

Outside of the fence, Little Jack saw one of Tank's bodyguards getting another pit out of the back of a truck. The truck had pens in the back which held six more dogs.

"The guards drive the truck full of dogs and Tank drives that new Buick over there."

Little Jack looked over to see the shiny new car CJ was talking about.

"Tank kills all his dogs that lose, and I get five bucks to bury them. We got to take them down to the lot. Too many dogs to bury in the yard. I made thirty bucks one night." Little Jack could tell that CJ was drunk by his speech, which was more than a little slurred. As Little Jack watched CJ maneuver the wheelbarrow, he wondered how many dogs he'd have to bury that day.

They buried the pit and when they reached the edge of the fence in the alley, they heard two .22 retorts. CJ looked at Little Jack with a drunken smile. "Five bucks," he said again.

The boys buried four of Tank's dogs. Little Jack had ten dollars in his pocket when the fights ended. CJ was pretty drunk. After the gamblers left and the boys cleaned up, they headed back to the pool hall.

"You're late," Blade said.

CJ and Little Jack had just entered the building. "At least I'm here," CJ said in his slurred speech.

"Ace," Rita said from her table. She waved Little Jack over. The boy named Todd glared at Little Jack as he approached. Little Jack noticed the glare and stared the bigger boy down before sitting at the table next to them. He noticed that two more girls had joined the group since he had left at noon that day. From the clothes that they wore, Little Jack guessed they were Kittens like Rita.

"Have you been here all day?" Little Jack asked Rita as she joined him. His mood was good because of the ten dollars he had in his pocket.

"No," she answered. "We had to go so Blade could hustle up some cash to play CJ tonight. There was a juvenile detective in here today with your picture."

Little Jack panicked. His expression and worry were well worn on his face. Sensing this, Rita put him at ease. "We told him we never seen you before."

"Thanks for not saying anything," Little Jack said, a little more relaxed.

"He said you weren't in any trouble, but we didn't fall for that. It's always a trick."

That sealed the deal for Little Jack. He was a wanted man and probably facing a lot of time in jail. "Thanks again," he told Rita.

"We don't tell in this neighborhood," she said with a smile.

Blade ended up winning his money and more back from CJ that night. CJ was too drunk to play straight. Little Jack helped his friend home and into the back of the truck.

Before he went to sleep that night, Little Jack thought of home. His heart ached with the pain and realization that he wouldn't be back for a long time, if ever. He wondered about Tara. "Is she all alone somewhere?" He thought. He cried when he pictured Tanya getting buried that day. Images of Mama and Grampa flashed through his mind and before the tears got a break, Cindy's beautiful face registered. As he thought of her, he cried harder than he had ever cried before in his life. When he was finally done, the pain was gone. The grief over and he was on his way to becoming a man.

Chapter 11

"**R**inger!" Little Jack exclaimed. CJ, Jack, and a couple girls were throwing some horseshoes on Little Jack's birthday. He was fifteen and doing surprisingly good for himself.

They were behind a little store/club that they rented. The boys had put their heads together since Little Jack was twelve and came to live in the city.

A few days after Little Jack came to live with CJ, he came up with an idea. "I'm putting these ten dollars on Pinky," he said one night before the fights started.

"Are ya?" CJ asked.

"Yep," Little Jack answered with a serious look on his face. He wanted to put it all on Pinky. He figured that if he lost, he could just make more the next time Tank came around with his dogs.

"Well.... if you do it, I'll do it," CJ said. "I ain't never bet on the dogs before." He hadn't either. Usually, he blew what money he made on beer and shooting pool. "It's my last five."

That night they won their bet. Before CJ had a chance to blow his stash, Little Jack pitched an idea that would start them both on their way to being the richest kids in the neighborhood.

"You notice how that kid sells them beers at the pool hall?" Little Jack asked. The boys were cleaning up after the fights and in the best of moods with pockets full of money.

"Yes," CJ answered, picking up a beer bottle. "He does that for his daddy."

"I know," Little Jack said. He picked up a couple of bottles and asked, "Do you think your Pops would mind if we sold beers at the fight?"

CJ's eyes lit up when he heard this. "Hell no, he wouldn't care," he answered. "At the least, he'd want a cut."

"Well, let's say we go fifty-fifty with this money that we made. That's a lot of beer."

"Let's go talk to Pops," CJ said.

The boys did and of course, Rick didn't mind. He didn't even ask for a cut. The boys' little money pot began to grow. Little Jack was the brains of the operation. He distributed only a percentage of the profits to CJ and himself. It wasn't long before the boys were dressed nicely, each with a whole new wardrobe, including a couple of suits and ties.

One night before bed, Little Jack came up with the idea to get a club of their own and expand. He saw the perfect spot two streets down from the pool hall that they usually frequented, and it had room for at least eight pool tables.

With the down payment in hand, the boys went to Rita who was old enough to put the building in her name.

Business was slow at first. All the boys had was a radio and only beer and cigarettes for sale. It wasn't long though, before the place was packed. One pool table, two pool tables, all the way to eight. Which was more than the pool hall down the street.

Little Jack's brains for the business kept the money pouring in. They enlisted the help of the Tigers to discourage people from going to the pool hall down the street.

One night, back at the house, Tank O' Cannon showed up to fight some of his pits. Rita always ran the club when the boys went to the fights. The boys buried three of Tank's dogs along with one of Ricks. When the fights were over, they were approached by one of Tank's bodyguards.

The burly fella said, "I heard you boys got a little club. Sell a lot of beer."

"We do alright," answered CJ.

"My friend knows your Pops pretty good," the bodyguard said, looking over at Tank. Tank looked over at the boys and nodded. "We know that if you ever got in trouble with the law, you'd know not to say nothin."

"Hell no, I wouldn't say nothin," CJ said. "I ain't no rat."

"Good kid. That's really good. We're gonna make you some more money. How would you like that?"

"How?" CJ asked. He looked over at Jack who was expressionless.

"We got beer and cigarettes. Cost you half as much as you're payin' now."

"Well, hell yeah! I like that," CJ said. He looked over at Little Jack and asked, "What do you think?"

Little Jack nodded.

"You boys gonna be there at noon tomorrow?"

"Yeah," CJ answered.

The next day a truck pulled up behind the club and unloaded. The passenger of the truck was the bodyguard from the night before. He gave an approving nod when Jack asked him how much he owed and then paid. The bodyguard probably expected them to pay on the next load.

THE YEARS PASSED. LITTLE Jack forgot about home. It was too painful for him to think about. He just blocked it out like a lot of people do that endure trauma of that nature. The boys owned three clubs now and a '41 Sedan that they used to collect their money and do business in.

"Six pack!" CJ yelled after Little Jack threw his second horseshoe. "That's game." Little Jack was to horseshoes what CJ was to pool.

"Happy Birthday," one of the girls told Little Jack with a smile.

The boys walked with their girls to the front of the club. They kept inventory on the beer and cigarettes and had a girl working in each joint. They were more trustworthy.

Both boys had their own dogs now too. They weren't going to cut into Rick's business. They always took them to Rick's to fight. They didn't live in the back of the truck anymore either. The second club they owned had a basement that they turned into a small apartment.

Life was good for the two teenage boys, who didn't even have their license yet. They didn't have to worry about the police either. Tank's bodyguards took care of that with a weekly kickback that the boys gave them. So long as they kept the fights down, they would have nothing to worry about.

The Tigers had grown in numbers and were the best customers the boys had. Little Jack, using his business sense, put Blade on a secret payroll to insure the peace. He didn't have to worry about the Tigers breaking away and forming their own clubs. Blade was too stupid and too busy drinking to ever pull that off.

At the front of the club, CJ, Jack, and the two girls pulled up chairs at one of the tables. A few minutes after sitting down, Little Jack was up and out of his chair before the others saw the car pull up to the curb.

"ACE," A FEMALE VOICE called out from the driver's seat. Rita got out of the car and gave Little Jack a big hug. One of the girls at the table was looking a little steamed until CJ said, "She's like his sister." That calmed the girl down.

"Happy Birthday!" Rita said after releasing Little Jack from her grasp.

"Thank you."

"You told me you were fifteen when I met you and I believed you."

Little Jack laughed when he remembered. Rita had since moved on to college and had to quit helping at the clubs.

"Another couple of years and we'll have to run off and get married," Rita laughed.

"You'll be an old maid by then," Little Jack chuckled and then backed up before she could hit him.

They joined the others at the table.

BACK HOME, THINGS WEREN'T so happy. Grampa, Denise, Tara, and Cindy knew today was Jack's birthday. Denise and Tara were at home. Cindy and Grampa were at the bar. The bond between them was so strong it couldn't be broken. Cindy was like the daughter the old man never had and Grampa was like the father she never had.

Grampa made sure the little girl went to school and ate right. Her mother had taken off last week, not to be heard from again. It was for the better, Grampa had thought.

HER MOTHER HAD BEEN gone a week now. Cindy tried to act strong, like it didn't bother her, but Grampa knew better. He had a heart to heart with the girl.

"How are you holding up, sweetie," They were sitting on the back porch after work.

"Fine," she answered. The sun had gone down, the moon was a quarter full, and there were so many stars, you couldn't count them all.

"Nice night," Grampa said.

"Yeah," Cindy said with a sigh.

"You know Cindy, you're welcome to stay on working here as long as you like."

Grampa sat quietly for a moment and then was startled as she burst into tears. "She's not coming back." She reached into her pocket and pulled out a note. It was crumpled and torn in some places. It had been well read.

Grampa Jack read the letter. His first thought after reading the note was, "How could anyone be so cruel?" The note was from Cindy's mother, telling her she raised her all she could. That she was leaving and wasn't coming back.

"Why does my own mother hate me?" Cindy cried.

"She doesn't hate you," Grampa said. He was trying to find the words to console her. "Cindy honey, some people don't ever grow up and some people just think about themselves. I'm afraid your mother falls into both of those categories, but that doesn't mean she don't love you. Do you understand what I mean?"

Cindy stopped crying and answered, "Yes."

"You're more grown up now than your Mama ever will be."

Cindy looked up at Grampa Jack and asked. "Do you really think so?"

"I wouldn't say it if I didn't mean it."

Cindy reached into her pocket and pulled out a bundle of cash. "This here is sixty-five dollars. I've been saving money here and there since I've been working. I want you to have it, for rent." She thrust it out to Grampa, but he refused to take it.

"No, you keep your money and stay right there in the house. I appreciate the gesture. That shows what I was saying was true about how mature you are." Grampa hadn't been paid rent on the house for so long he didn't care about the money anymore. His bar and other houses were enough for him to live good for the rest of his life.

Cindy smiled.

"Just do me a favor and don't tell anyone your Mama ran off." Grampa paused for a minute. He looked around his back yard, remembering the day Little Jack walked through, grabbing an equalizer for the Campbell's. "We don't want the child services people called and have them snooping around here again."

At the sound of child service workers, Cindy's thoughts turned to Little Jack. "I wonder where he is," she said.

"I don't know," Grampa said after a moment of silence.

Cindy went back to her house feeling better than she had all week. She decided that in the morning she would change the house around the way she wanted it and would take her mother's bedroom.

She got into her nightgown, said her nightly prayers, and climbed into bed. Looking out the window, at the moon she looked at every night before she fell asleep, she thought of Little Jack, as usual.

"Happy Birthday, Little Jack," she said, before going to sleep, "Wherever you are."

Chapter 12

Little Jack and CJ were at the second club that they rented; in the basement apartment they called home. They were up late the night before as usual.

"What time is it?" CJ asked. He was hung over as usual.

"Ten thirty," Little Jack answered, feeling rather good.

"My head is killing me," CJ said with a grunt. He sat up and rubbed where it hurt.

Little Jack looked over at his friend, amused. He never could get over the amount of beer CJ could drink. He always blew his money as quickly as Little Jack gave it to him. Little Jack was smarter than that. He kept a big percentage of his profits stashed behind a brick in the wall that he could pull out. He had a little over four thousand dollars in there and it was steadily rising.

"You've got a headache every day," Little Jack said.

"Nothing a little hair of the dog won't cure," CJ said, grabbing a beer and chugging.

The boys got dressed and walked down the street to 'Mom and Pops Diner.' It was a hot summer morning. The streets were packed with cars and people were walking along the sidewalks.

"Looks like a good day for business," CJ said.

"Every day is a good day for business," Little Jack replied. "People love to drink."

The diner was packed as usual. Before the chiming of the bells on the door could die down, as the boys walked in, a couple of girls were waving them over to a booth. Little Jack and CJ were quite popular, owning three clubs and all.

"The usual, fellas?" a tall waitress asked. She was delivering a plate of bacon and eggs to the booth next to theirs. The whole place smelled of food, things that Little Jack liked. CJ on the other hand felt as if he might be sick.

"Sure, Samantha," Little Jack answered.

The boys enjoyed their meals along with the company of the girls. CJ downed three cups of coffee that woke him up. Little Jack was happy not to hear about headaches anymore.

They said goodbye to the girls and left the diner. Outside, the heat seemed to have risen at least ten degrees.

"What do we have to do today?" CJ asked. He wiped sweat from his forehead and waved his hat, fanning his face.

"We've got to pick up a load of beer for Three Club," Little Jack answered. They referred to their clubs by numbers, One, Two, and Three.

"Let's go, man," CJ said.

The boys hopped into their car and drove deeper into the West Side.

The warehouse was Tank's. The boys had started picking up their own beer and cigarettes, once they got their own car. The workers knew them as regulars, so it didn't take more than fifteen minutes to do the usual hellos and chit chat while they loaded up.

The boys went back and unloaded the beer at number Three. They unlocked the place and let the girl in that ran the first shift. The boys then went to number One and opened it.

After being done with One and Three, the boys went to number Two. They opened all three joints at noon or shortly after.

Out in front of number Two, they relaxed and greeted teenagers as they came to socialize and drink beer.

"You know, we should be on the lookout for a number Four," Little Jack said.

"Yeah," said CJ.

"We can afford it," Little Jack said, taking a sip of soda, "more money would flow in."

"Sure thing. Have you thought of a place yet?"

"No. That's why I said we should be on the lookout."

"Well, we've got these three spread out pretty good," CJ said.

"Yeah, we'll have to make sure it's at a good location."

Enjoying the shade of the umbrella at the patio table, the boys jumped when a car screeched to a halt in front of the place. Rita jumped out.

Little Jack jumped up to greet her. His heart pounded when he noticed that her dress was torn, and she was crying. "What's wrong?" he asked as she ran into his arms, sobbing.

"Todd attacked me," she cried. Her makeup was smeared and her hair a mess.

"Did he hurt you?" Little Jack asked, furious.

"No."

"Are you sure?" CJ asked. He was standing next to them.

"Yes," she sobbed. "But he tried to do things to me. I told him I wasn't like that, so he slapped me and tried to rip my clothes off."

"Where is he?" Little Jack asked, angrily. "Where did this happen?"

"Outside, at number Three. I stopped there first to see if you were there. I didn't want to go out of my way to come here first if you weren't here."

Little Jack helped Rita around back and downstairs to his bed. CJ followed and listened as his friend calmed and soothed the distraught girl.

"I'm okay," she said after a while. She looked at Little Jack, her eyes red and puffy from crying. Embarrassed, she said, "I'm sorry I came to you crying."

"Don't be sorry Rita. That's what friends are for."

"I feel so silly," she said with an awkward smile.

"You're not silly," CJ said. "You're family."

Little Jack and Rita laughed at that.

"Thank you," she said. "I better get home."

"Are you sure you're alright now?" Little Jack asked.

"Yes, I'm fine."

"How long are you in the city for?" Jack asked. He knew she could only visit so often because of college.

"I'll be by tomorrow."

"Good, we can go to the zoo or something." Little Jack liked going places with Rita. She always had information on things that interested him. She was so educated and seemed to see things that Jack couldn't see until she pointed them out.

"Okay, Jack. Thank you, CJ."

"No sweat," CJ said with a wink and smile.

The boys walked Rita to her car at the front of the club. When she drove away, CJ said, "I'll get the car."

Number Three was packed when they pulled in. Little Jack slammed his door shut, followed by CJ.

Little Jack yelled, "Todd!" when he entered from the back. Todd was nineteen now. He had always acted like he didn't much like Little Jack. It was obvious that he was jealous of Jack and Rita's friendship, but he'd never given Little Jack a reason to call him out, until now.

The place got quiet when they heard Little Jack yell Todd's name. The smoke was thick as Patsy Cline sang in the background. Her angelic voice was the only sound that could be heard until Todd, with arms outstretched, asked, "What?"

"Outback! NOW!" Jack yelled. He made an about face, walking out the back door.

There were only three other Tigers in the building at the time. That made three and a half, counting Todd.

"Alright," one of them yelled with a smile, nodding his head up and down. CJ was glad to see him set down the pool stick he had in his hand.

Todd didn't look as enthused as his friend but tried not to show it.

Little Jack and CJ were waiting in the back when the four Tigers filed out of the club. There was enough space to park two cars, then the alley. All of it was dirt. The patrons piled out of the club, making a big circle around Jack and the others.

"Me and you, Todd!" Little Jack yelled.

Todd didn't get to answer. The happy fella from inside did it for him. "You mess with one Tiger; you get them all."

"You mess with the bull, you get the horns," CJ yelled.

Little Jack looked over to CJ with a puzzling look. He just shrugged his shoulders.

The four Tigers started cautiously walking towards the younger foes. The happy fella broke first and took a swing on Little Jack.

Little Jack saw the guy coming and blocked him with his left arm. He then smashed the boy in the nose. "Woo, it's been a long time!" Little Jack yelled, taking his shirt off as the boy staggered back. Blood poured from his nose like water running from a faucet. He didn't look so happy now and Little Jack was right. It had been a long time.

Seeing the trouble their friend was having, the other three approached a lot slower. Finally, one came at CJ and the other came at Little Jack. Todd stayed back, an obvious coward.

Little Jack stepped up and faked with his right. The boy fell for it and Little Jack hit him in the lip with a left jab.

CJ got close enough to his guy and started wind milling but kept his eyes open. He was whaling on the other guy, causing him to ball up. CJ grabbed his shirt with his left hand and started upper cutting with his right.

After taking the shot to the lip, Little Jack's opponent backed up. Little Jack followed through with a left right combination, When the right connected, that was all the other boy could handle. He hit the ground with a fractured jaw.

CJ finished off his guy. As he and Jack started to square off with Todd, Little Jack said, "He's mine."

"Get him," CJ said, backing up and breathing heavily.

Todd immediately started to back up, trying to get out of the fight. "No, you don't," Little Jack said. He kicked Todd in the groin so hard, the crowd moaned. Todd fell to his knees, holding on to his mashed privates, sucking in air that just wouldn't come.

Little Jack grabbed him by the hair. "Don't you ever touch a friend of mine again," he said, before punching him hard in the eye. "You know which one I'm talking about, don't you?" "Whack!" He hit him again.

Todd was dizzy but managed to answer. "Yes." Then said. "I'm sorry."

Little Jack punched him again and let him drop. "You are sorry," he said, disgusted.

"Everybody back inside," CJ said. He ushered the crowd back inside and managed to get the party alive again. When things were going smooth enough, CJ and Little Jack took off.

THAT NIGHT, BLADE WANTED to talk to the boys at Number Two. They were in the basement, counting money when he knocked on the door. Little Jack hurried up and put the loot away. The last thing he wanted was for Blade to see how good they were doing and get greedy.

"What happened today?" he asked as CJ let him in.

"What do you mean, what happened?" CJ asked back.

"You guys beat up four Tigers."

"So," CJ said.

"So, you can't go around beating up Tigers."

"Why not?" CJ asked.

"You just can't, man. Now all the Tigers are going to be after you."

"No, they won't," said Little Jack. He was sitting on a chair with his feet propped up on a coffee table like he didn't have a care in the world.

"What do you mean, no they won't?"

"They won't because you're going to call a meeting and get all of this straight."

CJ told Blade the story, starting with Rita, all the way up through the fight.

"That son of a bitch," Blade said. Blade and Rita were close, so this really made him angry.

He was sort of happy after he realized that he could clean all of this up. "We're gonna kick him out," he said with a smile. Yes, Blade was happy. He didn't want anything to mess up his beer flow and he loved his arrangement. If the Tigers ever found out about his secret pay, they'd definitely be at his head.

THAT NIGHT, NUMBER One was packed with an all Tigers meeting. Little Jack and CJ weren't there. They were at Rick's, fighting some dogs. They could care less about the Tigers coming after them. Sure, they wanted their business, but they didn't care one way or the other about a war.

Todd was tossed. Stripped of his jacket, he was shamed so badly, he couldn't fight the tears as his fellow comrades booed and jeered him down the street.

Chapter 13

Number Four was fine and making the boys even more money. Little Jack's stash was up to sixty-five hundred. The boys had the finest suits, ties and hats that money could buy. A lot of the older people were treating them differently now. Although they were always given their respect as hustlers in the past, it seemed as if now, they were looked on as equals to some, and above equals to others.

The Bulls was a secret name some of the kids and grownups started calling them after CJ made his remark at the fight with the four Tigers.

The boys had just opened number Two on a Saturday when a boy named Jimmy came in. It was twelve thirty and the only other person that was there besides the three boys was Carla, the girl who ran the club during the day.

The boys were sitting at a table, letting their meal from 'Mom and Pops' settle when Jimmy came up with an idea that would make them both do some serious thinking.

"I got a job at the beer factory on the East Side," Jimmy said while popping open his first beer.

"The distillery?" CJ asked.

"Yep, I load up the trucks, among other things."

"That's good," CJ said.

"Yeah, I load all the trucks and send them on their way. I know where all of them are going."

"That's good for you," said CJ, not catching the hint.

Little Jack knew what was on Jimmy's mind from jump street. It was common knowledge to the thugs in their circle that all the beer and cigarettes that they sold out of their four clubs was hijacked.

"How far in advance do you know when and where a truck is going?" Little Jack asked.

Jimmy made a happy face, realizing that Jack was on the same page as him. "The day before," he answered, then took a pull off his beer.

"What do you want on your end?"

"I figure a third," Jimmy answered. His and Little Jack's eyes glued to each other.

A light bulb went off in CJ's head and he felt a little silly. "Oh, oh okay," he said.

"Of course, you'll take care of the driver with your third," Little Jack said, his eyes still focused on Jimmy's.

"Yeah, sure. No problem."

"Meet us here two days from now with the time and route. We'll be ready," Little Jack said. He stood after he spoke and stuck out his hand.

Jimmy took Jack's hand after standing up. "I'll be here," he said and then walked out the door.

"I've never stolen anything," CJ said.

"Me neither," Little Jack pointed out. "But I've got it all worked out in my head. If he's got the driver in on it, there ain't nothin' to it."

"How are we going to do it then?"

"Well, I figure we buy us each a pistol and have Blade steal us a car the night before we go."

"Where are we going to put the stuff?"

"We'll rent us a warehouse." Little Jack was getting excited at the thought of all that free beer.

THE BOYS WENT OUT AND rented a warehouse that afternoon and then drove to Tank's warehouse to pick up some cigarettes. "We'll see if we can get the pistols here," Little Jack said as they pulled up.

Inside, one of the fellas said he had a couple and told them to meet him at a restaurant down the street.

Outside of the restaurant, in the parking lot, the man got inside the boy's car. He handed them a bag that contained two .38 snub nosed revolvers. "Keep it to yourselves," the man said. "Tank likes you kids, and I don't think he'd appreciate me selling you these." The man threw in a box of shells for free before he left.

Now, all the boys had to concentrate on was the car.

Blade was drunk when they found him at number Two that night. "We'll wait until tomorrow," Little Jack said. "We don't want him freaking out and running his mouth when we try and cut a deal with him to run us a hot ride."

"Yeah, you're right," CJ agreed.

The next morning, the boys stuck to their normal routine. When it came time to open, Blade was waiting outside of Two. "On time," Little Jack thought.

Blade was there because it was his payday.

The boys opened number Two for Carla and told Blade to come with them while they opened the other three joints. "How would you like to make an extra fifty bucks?" Little Jack asked as he handed Blade his weekly pay. CJ was driving. The windows were down and the cool breeze on the warm sunny day had all the boys in good moods, happy to be alive.

"Fifty bucks," Blade said, excited. "Boy, would I."

"You're gonna have to earn it," Little Jack said.

"Well, what do you want me to do?"

"We've got a friend of ours, needs a car delivered tomorrow night."

"A boost?" Blade asked but knew the answer.

"Yeah. Can you handle it?"

"Sure, just tell me where to park it."

"Alright," Little Jack said, reaching into his pocket. He pulled some bills off and handed them to Blade.

Blade eagerly counted the money. "Hey, there's only twenty-five dollars here."

"Half now, half later."

"That's fair," Blade said, pocketing the loot.

The next day, Jimmy showed up on time as planned. It was him, Jack, and CJ with Carla running around the place.

"Good to see you, Jimmy," Little Jack said, greeting his new business partner. "I hope you have some good news for us."

"Carla, bring Jimmy here a beer," CJ said.

"Who me?" Jimmy asked. "I'm always the bearer of good news."

"Good, Jimmy. Good." Little Jack said.

Carla dropped off Jimmy's beer and the boys discussed their plans. Jimmy handed over a crude drawing to the boys. Little Jack took it. "I got the driver," Jimmy said. "All you have to do is tell him to pull over."

"Good work," Little Jack said, looking at the drawn-up map.

"That's the route right there. All you have to do is follow the truck with the red cloth hanging off the driver's side mirror. The map's just in case you lose him."

"Alright, Jimmy," Little Jack said, still studying the map.

Jimmy had another beer and left.

"Well?" CJ asked.

"Well, what?" Little Jack asked back.

"What do you think of the route?"

"It starts on the east side and stays on the east side."

"So."

"If something were to go wrong, we wouldn't be able to get any help from Tank."

"Yeah, I see," Little Jack said. "We've got too much money in this thing to back out now."

"You're right," said CJ downing a beer. "Tonight, it is then."

"Yep, tonight it is."

THAT NIGHT, THE BOYS got into the car Blade left for them. They parked down from the distillery and waited until their truck pulled out. "There it is," Little Jack said. They pulled out into the dark night, following the truck.

As the truck stopped at the end of the street, Little Jack pulled up behind it, trying not to look too suspicious. When the driver turned right, CJ said, "It's going the right way."

Five minutes later, on a busy street, connected to a desolate street, the boys pulled up next to the truck.

"Pull over," CJ said, ready to show his gun.

The driver, looking about fiftyish with a fat, balding, brown head, nodded and obliged. When the driver got down, CJ climbed in. He drove off immediately with Little Jack on his trail. Little Jack was nervous for the first block. He started to calm down, everything was looking good. Things were going smoothly until they got about ten blocks away. That's when all hell broke loose.

First, Little Jack saw the flash of the lights, then heard the sirens. CJ punched the gas and shifted the gears of the big truck, pushing the engine to its limit like he was born in a rig.

Little Jack saw that three unmarked police cars were onto them. He slowed down, heart racing, and swerved from side to side, not letting any of them pass him. CJ was getting a bigger and bigger lead on them. After turning down two streets, Little Jack couldn't see the rig anywhere.

Knowing the route to the warehouse, Little Jack punched the gas into the stolen car. He fishtailed around a left turn, leading the officers away from CJ's location. The three cars were on his tail now.

He turned left again as his back window exploded. Little Jack didn't know what happened until he heard the gunshots. "The bastards are shooting at me!" he yelled. Pulling out his pistol, he fired back when he got on to a straight street. He quickly ducked down, leaving his head up enough to see the road. The officers fired back. Little Jack took a fast right and had the engine gunned full speed before he was halfway down the street.

Firing his pistol again, he was shocked when the lead police car swerved and crashed into the front porch of some unlucky bastard's house.

Determining to get away long enough to bail out, Little Jack took another sharp right. The other two police cars were on him. Halfway down the street he aimed to turn into a parking lot. As he turned all the way to the right, one of the bullets from the chasing police cars blew out one of his back tires. At the sound of the tire popping, Little Jack lost control of the car and slid. He balled up and braced for impact as the car smashed into a telephone pole on the edge of the lot.

The last thing Little Jack remembered about that night was seeing the police cars. He didn't wake up until two days later. When he did, he was handcuffed to a hospital bed and an officer was sitting in front of his door.

NO ONE KNEW THAT CARLA was Todd's girl. If they had, she wouldn't have held the position that she did. Hearing the boys' conversations, she phoned Todd. Todd, wanting his revenge, called the police.

PAUL DONOVAN QUESTIONED the boy to no avail. The kid said his name was Jack Gordon and that was it. He wouldn't say another word.

Detective Donovan swore the boy looked familiar but couldn't place him no matter how hard he tried. He'd dealt with so many kids and cases over the years, it was hard for him to remember them all.

IN FRONT OF THE JUDGE, the boy going by the name of Jack Gordon, didn't make anything easier on himself by not answering any questions. He didn't even flinch when the judge sentenced him to juvenile detention. His expression was blank. His eyes were those of a grown man.

TANK O' CANNON COULDN'T do anything for the boy. By the time he found out what was going on, Little Jack was on his way to a gladiator school.

Chapter 14

The gardens at The Stratton Detention Center for Youth went unnoticed as Little Jack rode through it's cold, iron gates. The nearly broken down, ragged state bus squealed to a stop in front of the receiving unit.

One would have thought the place deserted if not for the two correctional officers in front, waiting to greet Jack and the others to their new home.

Housing units were beyond the receiving center. All were made of Sandstone and kept well maintained.

Little Jack was far away from Stratton in his mind, until the bus door swung open, snapping him back to attention. He could tell that the boy sitting in front of him was incredibly nervous. He wasn't though. He was annoyed and mad at the world more than anything.

The fifteen other boys on the bus that day possessed thoughts of home. Desperately wanting to be back and swearing to their Gods with all their hearts and minds that they would be good this time.

"Gordon...Jack," one of the staff called out. His was the seventh name called. Stepping off the bus, Jack got in line with the others.

The fresh fall air was a relief after so many miles of burnt fuel he'd had to endure, not counting the time he spent in holding, waiting to finish with court.

The weather wasn't cold, but it wasn't all that warm either. It was more of a nameless, in between feeling. It didn't matter to Jack. He wasn't paying attention anyway.

After being deloused and given a bed roll, Little Jack and the new Fish were escorted to the chow hall.

The evening meal of roast beef, mashed potatoes, green beans, and dinner rolls was being served. The smell of hot food brought the awareness of their hunger to all the new inmates.

The loud chatter Jack had heard coming through the door stopped. All stared at the new Fish as they grabbed their trays.

Little Jack got his tray and picked a table. He didn't ask if he could sit and didn't look at any of the other boys as he did so.

The chow hall went back to normal. As Jack began to dig into his meal, one of the boys asked, "Where you from?" He was bigger and taller than the other boys at the table. Little Jack ignored him and kept eating.

"I said, where you from?" the boy asked again. Little Jack dropped his fork onto his tray. Everyone at the table quit eating. He lifted his head up to meet the eyes of the boy. He kept an icy stare locked onto him. After fifteen seconds of this, the bigger boy dropped his eyes to his tray. Looking around at the rest of the boys, he noticed that they too, had gone back to their meals. Jack ate the rest of his meal in peace.

After the evening meal, all of Stratton's youth were led outside. Little Jack found a seat, in the grass, far away from the bleachers where most of the others had gone. A softball game was under way.

Little Jack was studying the high fence and barbed wire that surrounded the grounds of his new home.

"It doesn't matter if you get over the fence," Jack was startled to hear a voice say from behind him. He quickly turned around. "It doesn't matter. All that is back there is cliffs and drop offs." The boy was tall, skinny, and missing his two front teeth. His red hair brought out the massive number of freckles that adorned his cheeks. "In front of this place is a river. You'd drown if you tried to swim across."

The foothills behind the institution didn't look like much to Little Jack.

"I've been here for four years now," the boy went on. "I've seen nine guys make it over the fence. I saw all nine of them come back too. Six of them on their own."

Little Jack, although not as annoyed at this boy as the one in the chow hall, kept his silence. During his silence, a light breeze brought the smell of the Mississippi to Jack's senses. He didn't even notice it on the way in.

"My name is Gary...Gary Vaughn."

Little Jack nodded.

"If you ever feel you need to talk, or if you have any questions about this place, feel free to ask."

"POP!"

Little Jack turned around to see that the crack of the bat had sent a ball flying into the foothills behind Stratton. The spectators and players of the game went crazy as Jack turned around to nod at Gary Vaughn again. It was too late. The tall, lanky boy was already walking away. His head was down, and his hands were clasped behind his back. He had the look of someone in deep thought or depression.

"LIGHTS OUT," A GUARD called. A few seconds later, Jack was surrounded by darkness. He laid bundled up in his top bunk, in the open, sixty-man dorm. As the chatter died down, his mind took him to a chopping block in his Grampa's backyard, and to a conversation with Cindy.

Chapter 15

"Everyone goes to school here at Stratton, Mr. Gordon," a big, bearded officer said Monday morning after breakfast. Jack had hesitated as the other boys filed out into the morning sun. A previous fog had lifted, leaving the dark green grass filled with dew.

Little Jack had awakened that morning after an exceedingly long weekend at his new home. A weekend filled with watching others play softball.

He'd noticed that the other Fish that came in with him had adapted immediately, joining in with the sports, trying to fit in by getting to know everyone.

Not Little Jack. He maintained his leave me alone attitude. Occasionally tuning in, he picked up on a few names. Rick for instance, was the name of the boy who had asked him where he was from at his first dinner. He could tell by the way the others crowded him and listened to what he had to say that he had clout. He was looked highly upon by the followers. What he noticed most about Rick was that he liked to stare at him. Sizing him up. Readying himself for battle.

"Everyone take a seat," the teacher announced when Little Jack entered the classroom.

She was a shockingly beautiful, full-figured gal. Tall with green eyes and flowing, light red hair that reached the middle of her back. She was the first woman Little Jack had seen at Stratton.

"For all of you, new guys, my name is Miss Sexton."

"Hi, Miss Sexton," the class said together.

"Let's all rise and say the Pledge of Allegiance."

When the Pledge was complete, all the new guys were given tests. "These will show me where to start you in your studies."

Little Jack, wanting to know where he should be in his studies, eagerly went to work.

LUNCH WAS NOTICEABLY quiet. Little Jack knew why. Rick's stare told all. His greasy, parted hair and gapped teeth made Little Jack sick. Both boys were two of the biggest there.

Outside, walking from the chow hall to the school building, another stare from Rick did it. Little Jack walked over, keeping eye contact the whole way. The other boys in attendance moved to one side and made a circle. Little Jack squared off with Rick and as the two boys circled each other, Jack's mind flashed to his Grampa's backyard. He took a stance he was taught. Rage and anger filled the young scrapper as the image of his sister, Tanya, flashed through his mind.

He attacked. "Swoosh!" A fake jab, followed by a left hook, both missed Rick. Rick laughed with his gapped teeth showing. He ducked another shot from Jack and landed a left and right jab. Both connected to Jack. He staggered back and shook off the surprisingly hard punches. He realized he couldn't win if he fought angry. So, taking a deep breath, he took another stance, readying himself for action.

Rick laughed harder, amusing the loud crowd gathered around them. He threw a right jab. Little Jack ducked and came up with a right upper cut. The upper cut landed on Rick's chin. Following through, and glad to have shut the laughing boy up, Little Jack squatted low, right jabbing Rick in the stomach. The boys in attendance gasped as he sent a hard, left hook to Rick's temple. Rick hit the ground hard, knocked out.

Little Jack, hardly winded at all, looked at the crowd and without words asked, "Who's next?" None of them wanted any.

The boys started to disperse. A couple of Rick's flunkies started to smack him awake and help him to his feet.

On the way back to class, Little Jack noticed the big, bearded correctional officer watching from outside of the control center. When he nodded approvingly to Little Jack as he passed him, Little Jack knew he had witnessed the whole incident.

The months flew by at Stratton. The fighting continued off and on. Rick got a couple of rematches but ended up with the same results. By and by, Jack noticed that he didn't have as many people hanging around him as he used to. Something that really ate Rick up inside.

By beating Rick, Little Jack had to fight every new tough guy that got off the bus, looking for a name.

Little Jack's only escape was school. As he studied and learned, he realized how big the world was. He often went back to his talks with Rita. From time to time, he wondered about her. How she was? Where she was?

When he lived in the city, it was as if the life he knew before was a dream.

Now, as the time passed by in Stratton, he began to feel the same way about the city. His thoughts dwelled more and more on his first home with Cindy, Grampa, Tara, and Mama.

Miss Sexton talked to Jack after class on occasion. When he'd started in her class, he was at a low, elementary school level. Now, after only thirteen months, he was ready to graduate. It had everything to do with him not having to wait for the class before he could move on with his assignments. At Stratton, each student moved along at their own pace.

"College is the key to a solid career, Mr. Gordon." How many times had he heard her say that over the last year? A hundred? No matter how many times, he never got tired of hearing it. It was as if she were trying to pound it into all her students' brains.

"You' re out of here in three months. Have you put any thought into your future?"

"Yes, I want to go to college, Miss Sexton." She was the only one he truly paid any attention to.

"What have you thought of majoring in, Jack?" She blushed when she realized that she called him by his first name.

Jack blushed also. His face turned crimson red as he looked at the floor and answered. "I haven't put much thought into it, Miss Sexton, but I think teaching would be nice."

Miss Sexton smiled at Little Jack when his eyes met hers. "You can be anything you want to be Jack. Just be sure about what you want to be. Think hard on it and don't limit yourself."

"I won't, Miss Sexton."

"Good."

Chapter 16

Eighteen years old and free at last. Little Jack felt nervous and fidgety as he walked down the Main Street of his hometown in Illinois. He had done his best to block the place out of his mind over the years. "Bad memories," he thought.

Main Street looked the same. Old man Black was sweeping the sidewalk in front of his hardware store. He looked the same to Jack. Wire rimmed glasses sat on the tip of his red nose. White hair around the sides of his head, the middle, bald and tan.

Jack walked past on the other side of the street. He wasn't surprised that Mr. Black eyed him suspiciously. Mr. Black would eye any potential stranger considering one ran off with his wife before Jack was even born. It was old talk in the small town.

The wind blew lightly, blowing Jack's hair back. As he passed the bakery, his stomach growled like he hadn't eaten in years. The smell of fresh bread and pastries reminded him of his belly's emptiness.

By the time he got in sight of Grampa's bar, he was anxious to see his people. Tough times forgotten, he walked in.

Hank Williams and the bells on the front door poured into his ears when he entered the bar. The smell of fried sausages and cigarette smoke filled his nostrils. The clanging of silverware and talk stopped as everyone in the bar looked at Jack. Jack's eyes were on the old man tending bar. His Grampa.

"Jack!" the old man yelled as he made his way around the bar.

"Grampa!" Jack cried out, meeting the old man halfway.

Grampa Jack and Jack met in the open area of the bar and hugged ferociously. Grampa eventually pulled Jack away. "Let me look at you," the old man said.

"Let me look at you," Jack said. The men's eyes were locked. "You haven't aged a bit, Grampa," Jack said as he stared at the old man with the bad knee.

"You have, my boy," Grampa said. "You have. Cindy, look who's here!" Grampa yelled back to the kitchen where things were still being clanged around.

Jack froze as soon as he heard Cindy's name. His heart began racing, beating faster than he ever remembered it beating all his life.

"Who is..." Cindy had started to say as she came through the door into the bar room. She had on an apron and was wiping her hands. When her eyes met Jack's, she froze for a second. "Jack!" she screamed. Tears rolled down her face. Tears of a grown woman, not the tears of a little girl. She came around the bar and took Grampa's place in front of Jack.

She looked so beautiful to him. He was lost in her eyes. Her long, blond hair was pulled back with a loose piece of her bangs, hanging down the left side of her face. Her cheeks rosy, red from the kitchen heat. They hugged tightly, Cindy sobbing into Jack's strong shoulder. "Where have you been?" she cried.

Jack didn't answer the question at first. He fought back tears. Savored her smell. Citrus and shampoo, some kind of perfume, splashed on lightly. He pulled her away. Delicately, he held her face in his hands. Locking his eyes to hers, he wiped away the tears with his thumbs. As he spoke, Cindy looked deep into his eyes, boring into his soul. "No matter where I was, or what I was doing Cindy, in my heart and mind, I was always here with you." Cindy thought she was going to melt. The voice that came out of the young man that held her face wasn't the voice of Little Jack Sampson. It was the voice of Jack Sampson, the man. They hugged again. Jack smoothed Cindy's hair.

Her head was still on his shoulder. When Jack looked over at Grampa, he could have sworn he saw tears on the verge of falling out of the old man's eyes.

"We've got to celebrate!" the old man said as he turned back to the bar.

Cindy pulled back from Jack. She smiled at him, a little embarrassed, as Jack smiled back.

The noise in the bar picked back up as the patrons took their turns giving Jack hugs, handshakes, and pats on the back. "You look good boy," Ed said with a big yellow toothed grin. Jack had grown into a town legend over the years. Some said he was dead, others told outrageous tales of adventure.

"Have you eaten?" Cindy asked.

"No," Jack answered with another smile. He was happy to be home and beginning to relax.

"Sit down here and I'll bring you the best breakfast you'll ever get in Illinois," Cindy said, pulling a chair out from one of the tables.

"She ain't lyin', son," Grampa shouted above the noise.

"No, she ain't," said Ed.

"Where is Mama and Tara?" Jack asked.

Grampa smiled and said, "They live over a hundred miles from here, but are on their way. They try to make it up one Saturday out of the month."

Jack found out that his Mama had remarried. He was shocked to hear it, but wasn't surprised by it, if it's at all possible to be one and not the other.

"Look who's here," Cindy said. Jack had already eaten and was talking to one of the townspeople who had come in to see him, once word spread around that he was back. A lot of people had come and gone.

Jack turned around to see none other than Junior Pratchett standing by the front door, staring at him.

"Jack!" he yelled. The sight of Junior surprised him. Junior was big as a little kid, but as a grown man, he was huge. Junior picked Jack up and swung him around like he didn't weigh a thing. Both men laughing like they were still in sixth grade.

"You got big, Little Jack," Junior said.

"Me! Look at you!" Both men laughed again.

Junior ordered a beer and as the early afternoon turned into late afternoon, the party continued. Jack didn't drink. He noticed that Cindy didn't either. It was obvious however that she was in charge of the place. Julie, the waitress, moved on to another town with her husband. Jack found out that she had been working there for years.

Ed and Junior were deep in conversation. Ed talking about the days he rode a horse to get anywhere.

The bells on the front door chimed for the thousandth time that day. Tara came through the door first, followed by Mama and some man Jack hadn't seen before. The place went silent. Tara looked like a princess to Jack. She was a beautiful young woman. Her hair, golden and curled. Blue eyes desperately searching the room. A man at the gas station had told them of Jack's return.

"Jack!" she screamed, running toward her big brother. She bawled as Jack embraced her. Hugging his little sister, he looked up to see his mother approaching him, crying.

HIS THOUGHTS FLASHED to Tanya. He noticed that his mother had aged but was still very pretty. He thought of his father as the man walking behind his mother came into view.

"I've missed you so much, Jack," Tara said.

"I've missed you too," Jack said as his mother joined in on the hug.

"Look at you," Denise said after they finally broke the embrace. She smiled at Jack with the tears of a heart sick mother flowing down her face. "You look so much like your father."

The strange man shifted a little at the comment and looked at the floor.

"Oh," Denise said. "I'm sorry, Christopher. Jack, honey, this is Christopher. My husband and you and Tara's stepfather."

"Jack," Chris said, sticking out his hand.

Jack shook his stepfather's hand saying, "Nice to meet you."

"I'm glad we finally get to meet," Chris said.

"Grampa," Tara yelled as she ran to the old man. The celebration continued in the bar.

Jack spent the early evening talking with his mother and sister.

AS CINDY CAME AND WENT, serving people their dinners, she caught Jack's eyes. They shared a look all evening, telling both they would talk later.

Eventually, Christopher said he was ready to leave. They wouldn't make it home at a decent hour if they didn't leave right soon.

Jack had learned that Christopher was a farmer and did well for Denise and Tara. They were happy. Jack was relieved. So many nights he had worried about both.

"Jack, you're more than welcome to come home and live with us. I could use a man like you around the farm," Chris offered.

"What do you say, Jack?" Mama asked.

Jack looked at Tara who was smiling. Her look told Jack that she wanted him to come badly. "I can't," he finally said. He turned his eyes away from his sister before he could see the hurt in them. Same as with his mama.

"I understand Jack," Denise said. "You're a grown man now. In a way, you've always been a grown man."

Christopher smiled at Jack. "Long as you know you're always welcome, Jack."

"I do and thank you."

"We'll be back to visit Jack," Tara said, her look reminding him of the happy little girl he once knew.

They hugged and said their goodbyes. Jack only shaking Christopher's hand. Not even trying to hug him.

THE BAR DIED DOWN LATER that night. It was decided Jack would stay in the spare bedroom. The same room that the family services people had had a problem with years ago.

Grampa had retired for the night, leaving Cindy and Jack to sit on the back porch and talk. Jack was thankful for the full moon that cast its luminescent light down on her. Her beauty was so great to him that he couldn't help but stare.

It was some time after Grampa left before they spoke. The crickets chirped. A few birds squawked or sang in the old oaks in the backyard, getting ready for bed themselves.

Cindy sighed before softly asking, "Where were you, Jack?"

Jack took a deep breath through his nose. He smelled Mother Nature in the night air, but what he smelled most was Cindy. He really enjoyed that. As he breathed out, he told himself it was a fair question. A question, when answered, would probably make him feel a lot better. So, he poured it all out, the words and story of his adventure emptied all the tension he had built up over the years. When he finished, Cindy stared at the moon, deep in thought.

"What did you do while I was away?" Jack asked softly.

Cindy told him of her mother leaving. She cried as she talked. She didn't bawl, just cried softly. She was a little hurt that Jack had the opportunity to write and say he was okay and didn't. "I thought of you every day," she said when was finished.

They talked for another hour. Cindy catching him up on the things that went on in their small town while he was away. Talking softly about those who died and those who had gotten married and had children.

As they sat side by side talking away into the night, Jack noticed that at some point during the conversation, his right hand had intertwined with her left. It felt good.

"Nice night," Cindy said after a moment of silence.

"There was a time when I wouldn't have noticed," Jack said.

"Really?" Cindy asked.

"When I was in Stratton, the leaves had changed and fallen without me even noticing. Someone told me after the fact."

"I believe that" Cindy said.

Cindy was lost in thought, staring at the moon when Jack brought her back with a question.

"Was everything fun when we were kids because we were young or was it because we just didn't care?"

Cindy squeezed Jack's hand and looked into his eyes with a sad expression. She sighed and said, "I don't remember having too much fun as a kid Jack."

Jack was saddened as Cindy's look and words absorbed into his brain.

She stood up. "I'm glad you're back, Jack Sampson." Reaching into a pocket on the front of her dress, she pulled out an envelope, kissed him on the cheek and departed.

He said, "Goodbye," and watched her walk through the backyard to her house.

When she was out of sight, he looked at the envelope. He cried as he took the letter out. A letter he had lost years ago, on a Sunday afternoon at his favorite spot. The last letter his father had ever sent to him._

Chapter 17

Days turned into months for Jack. He settled in nicely with Grampa, learning his trade. There was always work to be done.

"Wood's chopped," Jack said, coming through the backdoor into the barn.

Grampa looked through the window at Jack's work. "Damn son, that's three times as much as you used to cut and in half the time."

Jack smiled at that.

Cindy came in from the kitchen as Jack was sitting down. "I'll be ready in a minute."

"Take your time," Jack said, smiling at her. She smiled back.

Grampa smiled and said, "Picnic, huh? That's good. She needs to get out more."

"Ready, Jack?" Cindy had appeared with basket in hand.

THEY DIDN'T TALK UNTIL they were through Jack's old backyard. Cindy knew Jack didn't want to. Thoughts of Tanya were on his mind. And the bad memories, those were on his mind like flies on cows. As soon as they hit the timbers, all the bad went away. Being with Cindy these days was all Jack needed to be happy.

They had grown close. Attended a few dances. They were thought of as a couple. With Jack's good news, he had decided that this would be the day.

The warm sun felt good to Jack and Cindy as they wound through the woods. Relief and a sense of peace washed over Jack when he smelled the river. A light breeze bringing the scent of pines and fresh water.

"Look," Cindy stopped and whispered. She pointed out a fawn. The delicate creature was standing not ten feet away, a little ahead of them on the path. "So beautiful," she whispered softly, next to Jack's ear, taking his hand into hers.

Feeling Cindy's hot breath, Jack turned to look into her eyes. She smiled.

A Blue Jay squawked in a nearby tree. The quiet of the woods shattered by the sudden flight of two dozen quail. The fawn bolted on legs it wasn't fully acquainted with yet. Cindy laughed when Jack jumped. He laughed too as they continued to their spot.

Sandwiches and one of the best homemade apple pies Jack ever had were devoured quickly.

"What's it like in the city, Jack?" Cindy asked as she watched the water flow down river. He sat up against a tree, his legs stretched out on the blanket. She was lying on her side, her head resting on his thigh. He ran his hands through her hair as he contemplated his answer.

"It's a whole other world than here, Cindy. Neighbors are close. We could never be as comfortable as we are here, right now. There's nowhere like this in the city."

She thought about that for a minute and then wondered how anyone could not want to have places like this where they lived. "Jack?" she said after a few minutes.

"Yes."

"Did you have girlfriends?"

"Ha, Ha," he laughed.

"It's not funny Jack," she said and then asked, "Did you?"

"No, Cindy."

"Honest, Jack?"

"Honest, Cindy. I had girls that were friends, but no girlfriends."

Cindy rolled over onto her back. Moving her hair out of her face, she looked into Jack's eyes. Jack caressed her face lovingly. He took a deep breath, blew out, and began. "So, I uh, I got a job down at the lumberyard."

"Really Jack?" Cindy asked happily.

"Yes," Jack said as he smiled down at her, considering her to be the most beautiful girl in the world.

"That's wonderful Jack."

Jack reached into his shirt pocket, fishing around until he found what he was looking for, the engagement ring. He had taken it out of the box so Cindy wouldn't feel it and get an idea as to his intentions. He took another deep breath. His heart was racing, thumping in his chest. "Cindy?"

"Yes, Jack?"

"Will you marry me?" Jack asked the question smoother than he imagined he would. Grabbing a shocked Cindy's hand as he waited for an answer.

"Jack!" Cindy screamed, sitting upright. "Are you serious?"

Jack showed her the ring. "I've never been more serious about anything in my whole life, Cindy Ann Thompson."

"Oh my," Cindy cried, snatching the ring from Jack's hand, and placing it on her finger. "Yes, Jack."

"Yes?" Jack asked.

"Yes, Jack Sampson, I'll marry you."

"I love you, Cindy."

"I love you, Jack."

The engaged couple embraced. Gazing into each other's eyes before kissing deeply. The first real kiss since they were kids.

"WE'RE GETTING MARRIED!" Cindy screeched when she entered the bar.

"Whoa! Ha! Ha!" Grampa yelled.

"Look at my ring!" Cindy exclaimed, showing off her treasure.

People at the bar came up to shake an embarrassed Jack's hand. Grampa gave him a hug. "I knew this was going to happen."

THE WEDDING TOOK PLACE on a beautiful, Saturday afternoon. Cindy was breathtaking, dressed in white. Jack, cleaning up real nice in his tuxedo. Mama, Tara, and Christopher were there. Junior, standing tall as Jack's best man.

As they exchanged their vows, it seemed that all in attendance except for Jack and Cindy wept openly. Including Grampa and Junior. Even Reverend Jordan was teary eyed at the affair. Surprising, even to himself, after performing so many wedding ceremonies.

"Do you, Cindy Thompson, take this man, Jack Sampson to be your lawfully wedded husband?"

"I do."

"Do you, Jack Sampson, take this woman, Cindy Thompson, to be your lawfully wedded wife?"

"I do."

"With the power vested in me by the State of Illinois, I now pronounce you husband and wife."

"You may now kiss the bride." Jack lifted the veil.

THE RECEPTION WAS HELD at Grampa's bar. The honeymoon was to be simple; Jack was moving into the house next to the bar, with Cindy.

Grampa had offered to send them somewhere nice. Both declined. Just finally being together, as husband and wife, was enough for the couple. Whether they were next door or a thousand miles away, it didn't matter.

"I'll drink to that," Jack said to Junior. He was sitting at the bar, pretty buzzed up off his third beer. Cindy and the others were amazed to see Jack drinking. She wasn't mad though. Jack was trying to get over his nervousness. He knew what was going to take place once the reception was over.

The dancing died down and the party had pretty much slowed to a stop when the bells chimed on the front door, bringing a sight Jack didn't want to see, the Skinners.

"Well, well, well, if it isn't Little Jack Sampson," said Ralph Skinner. He had on a sheriff deputy's uniform. Standing alongside him was his brother, Tim, dressed the same. "We heard a while back, you were in town but was too busy to swing by and give our regards," Ralph said. Tim laughed, looking at Jack the same way he had back in school.

Jack, not wanting trouble on his wedding night, swallowed his pride and said, "Thank you for coming by."

"You're welcome, Jack. Thank you for being so kind," Ralph said.

"I don't think he's all that kind, Ralph," Tim said.

"Really Tim?" Ralph asked. "Why do you say so?"

"Well, he didn't invite us to the wedding. That's why."

"I gave out the invitations," Cindy belted out. All heads turned her way.

Jack's blood began to boil once Cindy got into the mix.

"You did the invitations?" Tim asked.

"Yes," Cindy answered, her voice stern.

"Well Cindy, I'm truly hurt," Tim said, pretending to be hurt by it. "After all we've been through, I thought we were like family."

"Like hell," Cindy said. The place grew even quieter.

"Thank you, boys, for coming out," Grampa said when he saw Jack and Junior, both standing up.

Ralph and Tim looked at the old man behind the bar. They could tell the Veteran wasn't in the mood for games. They knew he had a lot of clout in town and didn't want to be disciplined by the sheriff again. "Okay, Mr. Sampson," Tim said. "We'll be leaving now."

"Congratulations," Ralph said to Jack as he was leaving.

EVERYONE LEFT EXCEPT for Grampa and Jack. He'd said he wanted to talk to Jack before he left. Cindy went on next door to wait for her new husband.

"Jack, I understand that those two upset you and disrespected you on your wedding day."

"Yes, they did."

"I know it took a lot for you not to fight."

"I didn't want to ruin it for Cindy, but to be honest, whooping those two would have made my year."

"Ha, ha," Grampa laughed. They both sat there for a moment, enjoying the silence. Finally, Grampa spoke, and when he did, he was very serious. "Jack, if a man can't take backing down from a fight or losing a fight, then he has to kill." He stopped for a second to let his words sink in. "Son, there ain't much of a future in killing."

Jack was surprised at his grandfather's speech. "I reckon there ain't," he said.

"A killer spends the rest of his life being hunted, whether it's on the streets or in prison. Do you understand what I'm saying?"

"Yes Grampa."

"Good, now get out of here. Your wife is waiting on you."

Chapter 18

Jack came home from working at the lumberyard. He had been worried about Cindy all day. For the last three days she had been sick, throwing up in the morning. She hadn't been acting like herself either. To him, she had been a little standoffish and snappy. He'd racked his brain trying to figure out what he had done wrong, but for the life of him, he couldn't think of anything he'd done. "We've only been married for three months," he told himself at lunch.

"Cindy," he called out as he came through the front door, into the living room. He could smell fried chicken, his favorite, when she cooked it.

"I'm in here," she answered from the kitchen of their modest home.

Jack entered the kitchen as Cindy was getting the biscuits out of the oven. "Have a seat, honey," she told him.

Jack gladly did what he was told. Happy to see his new bride in a better mood.

She joined him at the table after washing her hands. Jack stared at her. She had the same rosy glow on her cheeks that she had the day he walked into Grampa's bar. She always had that glow when she cooked.

After Jack said grace, they both began to quietly eat. Fried chicken, mashed potatoes, green beans, and biscuits.

"It's good," Jack said, halfway through his meal.

"Thank you," Cindy said, already finished with her food. She always finished before Jack, probably because she ate half as much. She took pleasure in knowing that he enjoyed her cooking and always made sure he ate until he was full.

"You sound like you're feeling better," Jack said, after wiping his mouth on one of the cloth napkins. They had received them as a wedding gift from Rhonda.

"Jack?"

"Yes, Cindy."

"I'm pregnant."

"What!?"

"I'm pregnant."

"Are you sure?" Jack asked, barely containing his excitement.

"Yes. I had Rhonda drive me out to Doc Harold's office."

"That explains it all, Cindy. I mean, no wonder you've been sick. And me, all this time trying to figure out what I did wrong."

"I've thought I was for over a week, but I didn't want to say anything until was sure."

"This is wonderful Cindy."

"I'm sorry about my moods. I guess it's just part of the package."

"'That's alright, honey."

"You know, Jack, if you thought you did something, you should have just asked. We're married now. We're supposed to be able to talk."

"I know honey. I'm sorry."

Cindy got up and began to clean the table.

"Let me help you," Jack said.

"No, I'll get it. You probably want to go and talk to your Grampa. Don't you?"

"Yes," Jack said quickly and with a boyish grin. The grin made Cindy smile. "I'll be back," Jack said. He kissed her on the cheek and ran out the back door.

Jack entered Grampa's bar in the happiest of moods. Grampa noticed the strange look on the lad's face. He couldn't tell what it was but knew something good had happened to the boy.

"You're gonna be a great grandfather," Jack said, looking at the old man with a peculiar grin.

"What!?" Grampa asked. He wasn't sure he heard right.

"I'm gonna be a daddy!" Jack said. Then louder, for the whole bar to hear, he said, "You're gonna be a great grandfather!"

"What!?" Grampa screamed again. He knew he'd heard it right this time. "I'm gonna be a great grandfather!"

"Good job boy," Ed said with a pat on Jack's back.

"We've got to celebrate," Grampa said.

"Jack thought, why not, and drank along with his grandfather, Ed, and the other regulars at the bar.

"What are you gonna name it?" Ed asked.

"It's not an It, Ed," Rhonda said from a nearby table. "It's a child."

"Well, if it's a boy, I'm gonna name him Jack, of course," Jack answered. He was on his fifth beer and feeling a good buzz.

"Another Jack," Grampa said smiling.

"What if the child is a girl?" Ed asked, looking over at Rhonda. When he said, the child, she smiled.

"Well, in all fairness, I think Cindy should get to name her," Jack answered. Everyone in the bar voiced or nodded their approval at that.

"Ding!" the bells on the front door chimed. In walked Ralph and Tim Skinner, followed by Bill Campbell. The place went uncomfortably quiet. The boots of the two sheriff's deputies and their friend clicked on the floor as they made their way to the middle of the bar. It was the only sound that could be heard.

"What can I do you boys for?" Grampa asked when they stopped.

"Beers," Tim answered.

"Rhonda," Grampa said to his waitress. She obliged, looking a little uncomfortable. She knew trouble when she saw it.

Ralph, Tim, and Bill grabbed their beers and started chugging them. Tim spilled a lot of his down the front of his uniform. All three were drunk and out to cause trouble.

Jack didn't like seeing Bill Campbell. He knew George was dead, shot to death. And he'd heard Freddy was doing time up in Turndale, probably for the rest of his life.

"Little Jack Sampson," Bill said when he locked eyes with his old foe.

"Bill," Jack said with a nod, his voice stern.

"It's been a long time since the last time all of us were together," Ralph said, referring to the fight after school many years ago.

"Yeah, we're all grown up now," Jack said, trying to ease the tension.

"Yeah, Jack here just found out that he's gonna be a daddy," Ed said, wanting the troublemakers to ease up before things got out of hand.

"Really," Bill asked. "Who's the Mama?"

"He married Cindy Thompson," Tim answered for him.

Bill Campbell snickered. He was in the mood for a fight. He never gave up a grudge and, being freshly released from prison that morning, he knew he had to finish this business with Little Jack Sampson.

"Yes, they had a fine wedding from what I hear," Ralph said to his partner. "We wouldn't know though, because we weren't invited."

"Really," Bill said. He gave Little Jack a look like he wanted to kill him. "You know what's funny?" Bill asked Ralph and Tim.

"What's that?" Tim asked.

"What's funny is, when I was in the joint, Cindy came and obliged me with a contact visit and I'm probably really the daddy."

Jack slammed his beer mug on the floor, shattering it into a million little pieces. Ed jumped out of his way. Grampa walked around to the back of the bar, pushing Rhonda out of the way.

Bill Campbell laughed, taking a step back.

Jack stared at all three, his face beet red, his fists clenched. "You shouldn't have said that" he told Bill through clinched teeth.

"Oh really," Bill said, not scared one bit. He had become a dangerous man in the years since he last saw Jack. He had already killed four men in Chicago in different bar fights, always using a knife.

"Well, get it," Ralph said. He and Tim stepping aside.

Little Jack took off his coat. Bill took a step towards him. Jack took his stance and started to advance towards Bill. He told himself in his mind that he couldn't fight angry.

Jack took the first swing. Bill ducked and pulled a blade from behind him, slicing Jack across the ribs. The knife was sharp. Jack jumped out of the way, barely missing another slice.

"Make him put the knife up!" Grampa yelled at the two drunken police officers.

"Mind your business old man," Tim said, not taking his eyes off the action.

Bill advanced towards Jack. He swung the knife in front of him and would have gutted Jack if he wasn't so fast moving out of the way.

Jack bumped into a chair and quickly grabbed it. He swung it around to defend himself. Bill swung the knife again. Jack blocked it with the chair. After deflecting the shot, Jack lifted the chair in the air and cracked Bill in the shoulder with it, causing him to drop the knife. Jack quickly grabbed it and as he was coming up, he saw Bill grabbing a gun out of his sock. He had no choice, but to sink the knife into the other man as he started to point the gun.

With gun in hand, Bill Campbell was shocked to feel his own blade, the one he had killed four men with, sink into his chest. As he fell backwards, he fired a single shot and died.

The shot from the pistol almost hit Ralph Skinner in the ear but missed. Instead of hitting Ralph, the bullet found its way into Grampa Jack's chest.

Rhonda screamed and ran out the back door.

"You just murdered Bill," Tim said in shock and disbelief. Ralph didn't say anything. He just held his ear in shock as he stared at his dead friend, lying on the floor.

"Grampa!" Jack yelled. He ran to the back of the bar, holding his side, which was bleeding badly.

Ed started to cry.

Jack cradled his grandfather's head in his lap as he put a hand on the old man's wound. His own wound forgotten. "Talk to me, Grampa!" Jack said on the verge of hysteria.

Cindy entered the bar with Rhonda close behind. "Jack," she screamed. She ran behind the bar, not paying a tenth of a second's worth of attention to the dead Campbell laying on the floor.

"I took one in the chest," Grampa wheezed. Blood was coming out of his mouth, trickling down from both corners, dripping drops onto his neck.

Cindy grabbed his hands as Jack continued to hold his head. They both cried. "Grampa," Cindy sobbed.

"I knew the end was close," he whispered. "But I never thought it would be like this."

"No!" Cindy cried as the life left the old man's body.

Jack cradled the old man's head. Rocking back and forth, he groaned a grief filled, pitiful moan. Cindy put her arms around him. The weight of her grief almost killing her.

"You're in big trouble, Jack Sampson," Tim Skinner said. "You just killed Bill."

No one noticed that Ed had walked over and picked up Bill Campbell's gun until it was too late. "BOOM!" The gun fired, boring a hole through Tim Skinner's skull. His head snapped back, and his body crashed into the stools on the side of the bar.

Jack and Cindy jumped at the sounds.

Ralph Skinner snapped out of it in time to pull his pistol on Ed. He fired five shots into the old man. Ed never even had a chance to fire one off at Ralph. He knew he was the old man's next target.

"Everybody get where I can see them," Ralph yelled.

Slowly, Jack and Cindy raised up from behind the bar.

"Get out from behind there," Ralph yelled. He was breathing heavily and shaking like a leaf. "Tim," he yelled, looking at his brother out of the corner of his eye. His ears were still ringing from the recent blasts of his pistol.

THE TRIAL OF JACK SAMPSON was a joke. Ralph Skinner, being the police officer on the scene, painted a picture of Jack being a cold-blooded killer. He made the jury believe that he was the cause of the whole mess.

Jack's mind went blank when the verdict came in. Cindy nearly dying when he was found guilty and sentenced to life in Turndale.

Chapter 19

The sight of Turndale didn't scare or bother Jack. He could see the visible effects that the castle-like structure was having on his other bus mates though.

Once inside the sally port, a big, red bearded correctional officer entered the bus. With photographs in hand, he began to read off names. He listened carefully as each man said here, pausing after each one to make sure the pictures matched the faces that the voices came out of.

"This is Turndale. Your new home," the big sergeant began. "For some of you, probably most of you, this will be your last home. I don't know what other prisons you've been to, and I don't care. What I do know is that none of you have ever been to a place like this. There's not another place like this in America. If you plan on living very long, you better learn respect." The sergeant paused here and looked around the bus from face to face. Jack could tell that the big sarge had given this speech more times than he himself probably knew.

Off the bus, deloused and showered down, each of the new arrivals were escorted to the chow hall. The size of the place amazed Jack. The guards above the people eating held shotguns, ready to chalk one or two up for their team should a riot break out. To Jack, the food wasn't as good as Stratton's, but he wasn't all that hungry anyway. "I'll be here forever," he thought as he looked at his watery potatoes. All the population inmates had already eaten, which was a relief to Jack. He knew as soon as he landed, he'd have to be on the lookout for Freddy Campbell.

After chow Jack and the rest of the new load were given bedrolls and escorted over to the West cell house. The sergeant in charge of the cell house assigned the cells on the "Fish" tier.

The "Fish" tier was on one gallery towards the end. It was only the last ten cells with a gate dividing those cells from the others. Population inmates lived on the other side of the barrier.

Jack was assigned to a cell with a guy named Jonathan Sims. "What bunk do you want," Sims asked when the two were locked in.

"I don't care," was Jack's reply.

"Good, because I hate the top bunk," Sims said, sounding genuinely relieved. "I piss a lot at night and have been known to fall out of bed in the middle of the night. My brother's the same way. Broke his arm one time."

Jack stood in the middle of the room and absorbed only part of what Sims was saying. Stretching both arms, he wasn't surprised that he touched both walls at the same time. Even though the rooms were tiny, Jack thought it was better than those awful, open man dorms that Stratton had to offer.

"Small, ain't it?" Asked Sims.

"Mmhm," Jack answered.

The room contained the bunkbeds as you walked in, on the left side against the wall. At the end of the cell was a lonely sink and toilet.

Jack made his bed and sighed as he laid down. He was exhausted and ready to sleep. As he rolled his wedding band with the thumb of his left hand, he thought of home, Grampa, and Cindy.

CINDY WAS CRYING HERSELF to sleep at the same time. She'd done it every night since Jack was taken away. He possessed most of her daily thoughts. Grampa had left the bar and houses to Jack in his will.

Cindy ran the bar like she had since she was a little girl. She cried harder then, as she thought of Grampa Jack. All the years that she felt alone, Grampa Jack had always been there for her. She was three months pregnant and truly knew what it felt like to be alone now. Rhonda and a new waitress would have to take over when she got too far along.

JACK GOT UP AFTER SPENDING his first night in Turndale. He had total disgust for the entire world. As he and Sims stepped out of their cells for breakfast, the others on the tier stepped out as well. Three cells down from him, only one man stepped out.

"I killed him," he said to the group, his stare focused on the ceiling like he wasn't fully there.

"What?" Both men in the cell next to him asked at the same time.

"I killed him. Choked him to death. He liked to hurt children, talked like he was proud of it. I just let him talk until he fell asleep. Then...I choked him to death."

The bars racked that separated them from the general population. All the Fish, minus one, made their way to the chow hall.

Locked back down after breakfast, Jack heard someone call out his name. "Sampson." It was the voice of an old man.

"Yeah," Jack yelled down the tier. He realized the voice was coming from the population side.

"Was your old man named, Ace Sampson?" The voice sounding as if it desperately wanted him to say yes.

Jack waited a second. It hadn't even really dawned on him that this was where his father had died so many years ago. He looked around his cell and wondered if Ace had slept in the same very cell when he was a Fish at Turndale. "Yes," he answered.

"It's him," he heard the old voice echo out to someone on the same side as him. "I was a close friend of your fathers. Do you need anything?"

"No," Jack answered.

"Listen, you'll all be coming out of there tonight after dinner. I'm going to arrange for you to come to eight gallery with me and the rest of the fellas. When you get up there, ask for Pops. Did you get all of that?"

"Yes," Jack answered.

When they got back from lunch, Jack and the others noticed that the body of the dead man had begun to stink. "Guard," the man yelled that killed his cellmate. The guard turned around. "I'm not locking up in there."

"Why?" the guard asked.

"My cellmate is dead and he's starting to stink something awful."

"Everybody else, lock down," the guard shouted. "You," he said to the man. "Get up against that wall." He pointed to the wall across from the cells.

The guards came and took the man to the hole. Medical staff came and removed the body. An orderly was allowed in to clean the cell, but the stink lingered. Jack was glad when supper was over, and he was told with the rest to pack up and get to moving.

Eight gallery was a lot louder than one. He asked for Pops as soon as he was allowed to enter. An old man pointed down the tier and told him, Eight thirty-three. Jack made his way down to the cell; he himself was assigned to eight thirty-six.

"Sampson," the old man inside said when Jack stopped in front.

"Yes." he said.

"You look just like Ace," the old man said as he stood up. He was smiling ear to ear. He stepped out of his cell and took Jack's hand. "Tom," he yelled to someone a few cells down.

A man came out of the cell and looked Jack up and down. "Damn near identical," he said with a smile to Pops.

"Jack, this here is Tom. He was a close friend of your fathers too. You'll be living with him."

Tom walked over and shook Jack's hand. "Let me get that," he said, taking Jack's bedroll.

Jack found out what really happened to his father. He also found out that Freddy Campbell was in the hole for a stabbing. "Killed the man something awful," Tom had said.

That night, after writing Cindy a letter, he plotted his revenge as he lay in bed. He'd never be the same again.

Chapter 20

The first Saturday at Turndale for Jack really let him get rid of a lot of built-up tension. He pounded his opponents like they were schoolgirls. Warden Brown watched from a distance with a couple of his guards there to watch over him. He was amazed at the similarities between father and son. Dollar signs flashed in his eyes. The only difference he saw in this younger version of Ace was the eyes. The eyes of the son were those of a bloodthirsty animal. Each opponent he faced was as if he was trying to kill them with a single blow.

Out on the yard after the matches, Jack sat with his new friends and talked about some serious matters.

First was that of getting his blade. He'd asked Tom and Pops if they could get him one on his first night. He wanted to be ready to deal with Freddy as soon as he was released from the hole, which was rumored to be on Monday.

Second was when and where he should take care of his business.

"You killed his brother, huh?" Tom asked.

"Yes, I had too."

"I'd say the best time and place," Pops said, "would be right when they let him out. I'll find out what tier he'll be on. You're already on the plumbing crew with me. All we have to do is go up and say we are checking the sinks for leaks."

"Sounds good," Tom said.

"I'll keep the guard busy. You take care of your business. Just make it short and as quiet as you can."

Saturday after dinner, Warden Brown sent for Jack. Jack had seen the warden watching his matches and thought he might call him in.

Especially after the way Pops said no one had fought like that here since his father.

"Have a seat," the warden said to Jack as he entered the office.

Jack looked at the walls while he waited for the warden to finish his paperwork. It was full of photos of other wardens. Some were on horseback. He figured that Turndale used to be a lot worse back then.

"So," Warden Brown said after a few minutes, "I get the pleasure of meeting, Ace Sampson's son."

"It's a pleasure to meet you, Warden."

"It's a shame, what happened to your father. He was the greatest fighter I've ever seen...Until today."

"Thank you," Jack said.

"You have a lot of time to do, Jack. Do you think you can beat your fathers record of five Big Saturdays in a row?"

"I'm going to give it my best, sir."

"Good. And, as you try your hardest to complete that goal, I'll make sure your stay here is as comfortable as I can make it. All you can eat, special gym time for training while the rest of the inmates are locked in for count.

"Thank you, Warden."

"Alright, if you need anything, you be sure to let me know."

When Jack left the warden's office, Warden Brown was convinced that Jack didn't think that his father's demise had laid in his hands. Again, the dollar signs were flashing in his eyes.

MONDAY MORNING, POPS told Jack to come with him. They were at the plumbing shop, and it was right after breakfast. "He's on three gallery," Pops said, leading the way.

"Good," Jack said. "I'm ready to get this over with."

"Try your hardest, son," Pops said. "I got to see the parole board at eleven."

"What!?" Jack asked, taken back.

"I've got to see the board."

"Really?"

"Yeah."

"You shouldn't be in on this, Pops," Jack said.

"Don't worry about it, they aren't going to let me out anyway."

"How do you know?" Jack asked.

"I just do. They shoot me down every time."

They made their way to three gallery. The officer in charge was in control of two galleries, one and three. The cell house was divided in half. One, three, five and seven on one side. Two, four, six, and eight on the other.

Pops told Jack that Freddy was in three twenty-two before they were in earshot of the officer.

"Pops," the guard said. "What brings you up this way?"

"Got to check the sinks for leaks and such."

"There's plenty of them," the guard said.

"If you can, rack the bars and let him check up here and I'll check the ones downstairs. I don't want to be here all day. I've got to see the board later."

"Really?" the guard asked as he racked the cells on Three tier. Most of the inmates were at their jobs, so he wasn't worried about the place flooding with convicts. He had Freddy Campbell down there, that just got out of the hole, and Jonathan Sims, a new guy on a medical lay in. "You've been here forever, Pops," the guard said as he and the old man walked off to One tier.

Jack looked down the range. He slumped down to his work bucket and came out with the bone crusher that Pops had provided for him. He was halfway to Freddy's cell when he saw him look down the tier at him. Both men had death in their eyes. Freddy stepped off onto the tier, brandishing his own piece. "I got word that you were here," Freddy said in a hateful voice.

Jack ignored him and kept walking.

"You killed my brother."

Jack stopped two feet away, stepped sideways and began to inch his way towards Freddy.

Freddy turned sideways and did the same.

Jack slashed first, missing. Freddy sliced Jack's arm, as it barely missed his face. Jack felt the pain but didn't let go of the knife. He knew the cut wasn't bad.

Freddy kicked at Jack. Jack blocked the kick with his own foot and ducked as Freddy swung his rusty blade, almost hitting Jack in the throat. Jack came up fast and ran his steel in between Freddy's ribs on his right side and quickly grabbed hold of the wrist that held the knife. He shoved Freddy hard up against the bars and held him there as he jabbed the knife in and out.

Blood covered both men as the life left Freddy Campbell. Jack dragged Freddy back into his cell and laid him in his bunk. He covered him with a blanket and stepped back out. He quickly took his shirt off and wiped as much of the blood up off the gallery as he could before making his way back down to his work bucket. As he passed cell number three thirteen, he saw Jonathan Sims staring at him, shaking, and scared.

"You didn't see nothin," Jack said as he passed by.

At his work bucket, Jack stripped out of his pants and changed into the extra outfit he had inside. The old clothes and the knife he shoved inside an empty cell. He worked on regaining his composure as he waited for Pops to come back with the guard.

Chapter 21

Pops was denied parole. He wasn't too surprised. Neither were the other fellas. They were used to Pops getting shot down every year.

Jack and Pops were never questioned about the Freddy Campbell murder. Pops said it was because the warden didn't want to upset his new champion. Warden Brown hadn't had a fighter like him in years.

"What was my father like?" Jack asked Tom. They were lying on their bunks. Jack was tired after fighting five guys earlier on in the afternoon. They both had planned on getting up for church service over in the chapel the next morning.

"He was a lot like you, Jack," Tom answered after thinking about it for a minute. "He talked about getting out there to you, your sisters, and your Mama all the time. It's a shame what happened."

Jack was quiet for a minute. He went back to the past, to a Sunday morning years ago. He was proud of his daddy for not throwing the fight.

Jack fell asleep. In the morning, he awoke to the usual noises a prison had to offer. He brushed his teeth, combed his hair, and joined the others for church. After the service, he was surprised when a guard informed him that he had a visit. The fellas were happy for him as he hurried off.

"Jack," Cindy cried when he walked into the visiting room. Jack rushed to her with open arms. He hugged and kissed her, wishing he never had to let go. She cried into his shoulder as he rocked her back and forth.

"I've missed you so much," Jack said as he took a seat at the table, sitting across from her.

"I've missed you too, Jack," Cindy said. She was still crying. The nervousness she felt as she entered the prison was gone now that she was with Jack. She was happy that he didn't pay much attention to how big her belly was getting. Something she had been self-conscious about.

"How is everything going?" Jack asked. He'd spent nights worried sick as to how she was getting along.

She wrote often enough, but just because she said everything was fine in the letters, didn't mean things were so.

"Everything is fine back home. I hired a new waitress to help me and Rhonda out. She has a way with the customers."

"That's good."

"Julie came back for a visit. I put her and her husband up for a week. It was nice having someone around. She still couldn't believe Grampa was gone."

"He's in a better place now, Cindy."

"Do you think so?"

"I know so."

"Rhonda and Stacy, the new waitress, are going to run things when I get too far along."

"Good," Jack said. "How are you feeling? What does Doc Harold say about the baby?"

"The baby is fine. It seems to be very healthy. Three more months to go," Cindy said and then started crying again. She imagined the baby being born without Jack being around. She didn't want to raise it on her own.

"Baby, don't cry," Jack consoled, taking her hand in his from across the table.

"I'm sorry Jack," Cindy said, wiping the tears away with her free hand.

Jack smiled at her. Trying to make her be strong. He knew it was hard for her. "Listen, I want you to do something for me."

"What is it, Jack?"

"I need you to go to Chicago for me and visit an old friend of mine. Give him a message for me."

"Chicago, Jack?"

"Yes Cindy, Chicago."

BIG SATURDAY ROLLED around. Cindy was due to have the baby the next week. From a letter she sent Jack months ago, she confirmed that she had indeed contacted his friends.

"You ready?" Pops asked. Jack was in the locker room, preparing for his match. His was the main event, the same as his father's had been.

"Let's go," Jack said.

He made his way to the ring. The crowd in the gym went crazy when they spotted him. Chanting and cheering. Jack looked around the spectators and was happy to see Tank O' Cannon and CJ O'Reilly sitting close to the Warden's box. Tank's bodyguards were close by, scanning the scene. CJ looked good, decked out in an expensive suit. When their eyes met, they exchanged recognition, then quickly diverted their eyes.

Jack entered the ring and stared at his opponent. The man was big, but not as big as Jack. He kept his eyes locked as he made his way to the middle of the ring.

"I want a clean fight fellas," the ref began. "No rabbit punches. When I point to your corner and tell you to get there, that's what you better do. Do you understand?"

Both men nodded their agreement.

"Now, shake hands."

Jack and his opponent touched gloves and went back to their corners.

"They never used to do all of that back when your father ruled this ring," Pops said with a dry laugh. "It was just get in there and get it."

"DING!" The bell for round one sounded. Jack and his opponent went after each other. Jack swung first with a left hook, then ducked, and connected a right jab. The opponent countered with a left-right combination. Jack danced back.

He came back in with a double right, both connecting. The opponent dodged and weaved, got in a rib shot and bounced back out of the way before Jack could connect a hard, left-handed power punch.

"Ding!" Round one was over.

Jack made it back to his corner. He was hardly winded. He used round one to size up his opponent. The man had a lazy eye that was unnerving to Jack. In his assessment of the round, Jack decided that the man was well trained and used that round to size him up as well.

"You all were even on that one, Jack," Pops said, spraying some water into Jack's mouth. "Spit," the old man said, feeling more alive than he had since the last time he was a corner man.

"Ding!" Round two kicked off with Jack and Lazy Eye battling like their lives depended on it. The noise in the gym was at near, eardrum shattering proportions. Lazy Eye danced around, trying to avoid a hard punch from Jack. Jack was used to fighting people who fought more on the defensive. The few fighters he had faced that were aggressive, went down pretty quick when he put the heat on. Lazy Eye came in, faked with a left, and brought a right. Jack ducked the right and countered with a hard left, just as round two ended.

Back in his corner, Jack looked up towards Warden Brown. The Warden smiled down at Jack, his greed shining through his teeth.

Pops was chattering away about, faking with a left. Which is what Lazy Eye had just done. Jack knew what he had to do in round three. As he sat on the stool in his corner, he blocked out Pops and the rest of the noise in the gym. His Grandfather's words came back to him.

"Jack, if a man can't take backing down from a fight or losing a fight, then he has to kill. Son, there ain't much of a future in killing. A killer spends the rest of his life being hunted, whether it's on the streets or in prison. Do you understand what I'm saying?"

"I understand, Grampa," Jack said as the bell sounded, beginning round three.

"ACE! ACE! ACE!" Pops shouted. The rest of the crowd joined in. Warden Brown looked worried.

Jack went at Lazy Eye with his gloved hands held up, ready for action.

"Don't forget the left!" Pops shouted above the roar of the crowd.

Lazy Eye went at him. He dodged and weaved as Jack threw a mixture of combinations.

As Jack swung a right hook, he knew he'd come too wide. Lazy Eye took his chance. He blocked with his left hand and came through with a power, right hand to Jack's exposed jaw.

There was a flash in Jack's head as the lights went out. "BOOM!" He hit the canvas.

The ref ordered Lazy Eye to his corner. "ONE! TWO! THREE!"

"Get up," Pops screamed.

Warden Brown stood up. His eyes were bugged out of his head. His glasses began to mist as he breathed heavy, face red, sweat pouring from his forehead.

Tank and CJ were glued to the ref's count.

"FOUR! FIVE! SIX! SEVEN!"

Lazy Eye started bouncing up and down in his corner with his hands up in the air.

"EIGHT! NINE! TEN! YOU'RE OUT!"

Pops jumped into the ring and ran to Jack's side as people in attendance stared at the sight in shock.

Warden Brown was trying to get out of his box, but Tank's bodyguards were in the way, arms folded, shaking their heads with a firm, no.

CJ and Tank shook hands, smiling.

Warden Brown disappeared that night, never to be seen again. The rumor was that he'd bet more money than he had on Jack Sampson. They said that he met his fate in an Irish neighborhood in Chicago, torn to pieces by some real mean pit bulls.

Chapter 22

Word on the yard was the game was the same as when the elder Jack Sampson fought his last match at Turndale. They said a vessel in Jack's head busted from the fight.

Pops thought of this as he walked to the fence on the outer perimeter of the yard that separated the men from the wall. He spit out a nice hunk of chew spit as he began to climb. He was near the top when he heard the guard call out from the tower.

"Get down or I'll shoot!"

Pops just kept going. As he reached the top of the fence, the first shot rang out. He felt a burning in his back and almost let go, his left hand slipping.

He grabbed back on, tightly. He was at the top of the fence when the second shot hit him in the left shoulder. He grunted but kept on. Balancing himself on top of the fence, he grabbed onto the top of the wall. As he pulled himself up to the top. The third shot blew him over the wall. He crashed down hard on the other side of Turndale. The fall didn't render him unconscious. He laid on his back, fighting for air, bleeding to death with a smile on his face.

Pops knew when he tried to climb the fence, he was a goner. He just wanted to die on the other side. He wasn't sentenced to life in Turndale, therefore, he granted himself early release. He saw a flock of geese fly over as he fought for his last few breaths, listening to the loud alarm horn blast throughout the prison. As the lights went out forever for the old man, the smile remained.

BACK AT GRAMPA'S BAR, Cindy was ready to go into labor any minute. She was in a state of grief she had never experienced in all her years. Word had hit town of Jack's untimely death. Rhonda was holding her, terrified. She'd never seen anyone this distraught and being with child to boot. It was almost more than she could handle.

The bells on the front door rang as a group of men entered the bar. Cindy looked up to see the friend Jack had sent her to visit, CJ O'Reilly. There was a man with him who had an aura of power. Behind him were two big fellas that looked to be some kind of bodyguards.

"Why are you crying?" CJ asked Cindy as the bells on the door chimed again.

"Jack!" She cried when she saw him come through the door.

"I went to see if you were home first," Jack said as he ran towards his wife, sweeping her up into his arms.

"I knew you were going to throw the match," Cindy said when things calmed down. "It's just, when I heard you were dead, I thought something horrible went wrong."

Cindy was holding an ice pack on Jack's swollen, left eye. She now knew the story in its entirety. Pops knew too. His decision to die a free man didn't have anything to do with Jack. The guards at Turndale set the old man's body back inside the prison. In their report, they stated that he had fallen back inside the prison. They never wanted anyone to say that someone could make it over the wall at Turndale, dead or alive.

The bells on the door chimed again. Cindy was facing the door, a look of terror on her face. Jack knew who had entered.

"What in the hell are you doing out of prison?" Ralph Skinner shouted from the door. He had just come over to rub in the fact that Jack was dead. Angry, he began to pull his pistol.

He was too slow. Tank drew on him quicker than anyone could bat an eye. "Get this guy out of here," he said to his bodyguards. "Make sure he don't come back." Tank's voice was deep and serious. Jack was amazed to hear the man speak, let alone give an order of such magnitude.

The bodyguards did what they were told to do. One disarmed Ralph, and before he could scream, the other one conked him on the head with the butt of his revolver.

The bar calmed down after that. "I almost forgot," CJ said, reaching into his pocket. He pulled out a huge wad of cash. "I put the money from your stash spot against you, just like you asked. I couldn't believe my ears when Cindy told me where to look for it. I hadn't been there in years, but there it was." He handed Jack the bundle.

"Thank you," Jack said, taking the small fortune. He was very thankful that his friends, using their influence, were able to successfully fake his death. That part of the plan was not known to him until after the fight, when he was carted out of the prison on a stretcher.

"Jack?" CJ asked.

"Yeah."

"What say you come and fight for me and Tank? Make a lot of money."

Jack looked at Cindy. She looked back at him, very scared, with childlike eyes. "Nah," Jack answered with a smile. "I'm going to college."

Tank and the crew from Chicago left. The next morning, Cindy went into labor. She gave birth as Jack paced back and forth in the waiting room.

She was relieved to have a healthy, baby girl. "I'm going to name her Jacky," she said to the nurses as she held her wailing treasure.

Don't miss out!

Visit the website below and you can sign up to receive emails whenever Michael Neece publishes a new book. There's no charge and no obligation.

https://books2read.com/r/B-A-AGRN-RDPMB

BOOKS 2 READ

Connecting independent readers to independent writers.

www.ingramcontent.com/pod-product-compliance
Lightning Source LLC
Chambersburg PA
CBHW061536120726
48001CB00004B/1584